ASSASSIN TRAIL

Civil War ended and Major Tim
Cord led his band of hoodlums west to
cattle trails, intending to steal a herd to
in Topeka, and to move on to Huggett,
ebraska, to dispose of the loot amassed
ing the war. As Sheridan's Light Horse,
Cord's troop had brought terror to the
ilies of Southern landowners. They came
o of the night, killing all males regardless of
using all females, plundering valuables
transporting the best to their cache in
raska. Then at Waco they tangled with
e Grant!

ASSASSIN TRAIL

ASSASSIN TRAIL

by

Hal Jons

The Golden West Large Print Books
Long Preston, North Yorkshire,
BD23 4ND, England.

British Library Cataloguing in Publication Data.
_____

Jons, Hal
    Assassin trail.

    A catalogue record of this book is
    available from the British Library

    ISBN   978-1-84262-890-4 pbk

First published in Great Britain in 1981 by Robert Hale Ltd.

Copyright © Hal Jons 1981

Cover illustration © Michael Thomas

The moral right of the author has been asserted

Published in Large Print 2015 by arrangement with
Hal Jons, care of Mrs M. Kneller

The Golden West Large Print is an imprint of Library Magna
Books Ltd.

Printed and bound in Great Britain by
T.J. (International) Ltd., Cornwall, PL28 8RW

ONE

Steve Grant pushed wide the batwing doors of the Longhorn Saloon with a smile of anticipation on his lips. It was his first time in Waco for five years, and the thought of a long drink in congenial company had been with him a long time.

There was company aplenty, but not by any stretch of imagination could it be called congenial. Just a few oldsters looked morosely into their glasses, their faces stirred memories, but the other twenty or so taking up the tables were hard-faced, hawk-eyed men, all button-lipped and watchful.

The only friendly face belonged to Red Harman, who at that moment straightened up from seeking something behind the long bar. He stuck out a gnarled hand in greeting, but smiling came hard.

Steve thought Red had aged some. His hair was now mostly grey, and worry lines were deeply engraved on his face. His greeting was warm though.

'Good to see you, Steve! It's been a long time!'

'It sure has.' Steve turned and gave the customers a comprehensive glance before looking back at the barkeep. 'Not a face I know, Red. Where's everybody?'

Red Harman poured out a generous slug of bourbon and pushed it across the counter. He waved away the money Steve placed in front of him. 'You're the first back, Steve. Leastways the first whole man. A few have dribbled back through the years short of an arm or leg or broken up one way and another, but none of your old pards.' Steve nodded his understanding before taking his first taste of bourbon in a long time. 'Not that there's much to come back for,' Red continued. 'Things couldn't be worse. The bottom's fallen out of the cattle market. The critturs are near standing shoulder to shoulder wherever there's graze, and the last price Mellor of the Lone Diamond got down at Galveston was two and a half dollars a head. Most folk are talking of heading north to Wyoming, Dakota and Nebraska.'

'They'd do better to keep their homesteads, Red, and drive their cattle north to look for better markets. I've heard there are good prices paid at Topeka.'

'Hey you! Barkeep! You gonna palaver all day?'

Both Red and Steve looked across to the far corner table at the heavy-looking, bearded man who stared back at them, empty bottle in his hand.

'Fetch me another bottle, and look lively!'

The man's eyes were cold. Red Harman drew himself upright and stared back.

'I don't fetch and carry, Mister. I just serve those who can make it to the counter.'

The heavy-looking man stood up slowly. 'I just changed your rules, barkeep! You fetch me another goddamned bottle or I'll put a hole in your forehead!'

Steve groaned inwardly. As he remembered, Harman fetched and carried with the best. He also remembered that once driven Red was as stubborn as any mule. He gave the customers an overall glance and saw that every cold eye was on the barkeep. He found no cause for comfort, not one shred of compassion showed on any face.

'Can't see that'll help you any, Mister,' Red replied slowly. 'You salivate me and you'll still have to fetch a new bottle.'

'Nope, that's not so,' the man said without heat. 'That feller you're so all-fired friendly with will fetch it when you hit the deck.'

All the bonhomie left Steve Grant's face, leaving it severe. His grey eyes glittered as he spoke. 'You're setting your sights higher than you know, Mister,' he said evenly. 'You try throwing lead and you're a dead man.'

The black-bearded man looked unimpressed, and the other two men at his table moved away.

A long minute passed with the two men eyeing each other motionlessly, then Blackbeard went for his gun. It was still holstered when his throat exploded in a red gout of blood, and he fell forward across the table which spun away under his weight.

Steve Grant stood with the counter at his back, a gun in each hand, the left one wisping smoke from the barrel. He eyed the assembled company bleakly. 'Anyone else demanding table service?'

'No, Mister, there'll be no more table service. They'll be drinking up and on their way.' The speaker stood up, and held Steve in a magnetic gaze out of jet-black eyes. He was dressed in Scout's garb and looked a born leader. Tall, handsome, with a teak-hard, lithe body, and cruelty seemed to emanate from every pore. His two companions at the table sat easy, unshaken, the one slim, blond, sardonic, the other a ginger-haired giant of a man with a bland, expressionless face.

Nonchalantly, the speaker made his way to the bar, fished in his pocket, and tossed some coins on the counter, addressing himself to Red Harman. 'Enough there to bury the blamed fool good, and buy you a couple of bottles. Write out T.S. Shafter on his cross. He asked for it and got it.' He turned to appraise Steve again. 'I'd like to know the name of the hombre who could beat Shafter by such a margin.'

'The name's Steve Grant,' replied Steve quietly, still watchful.

The man stuck out his hand, and Steve felt the iron strength of his grip. 'Tim McCord,' he said, then when Steve nodded, he turned around peremptorily and waved his men out. Without demur, the men drained their drinks and made for the doors. McCord nodded again to Steve and followed them outside.

Steve let out a pent-up breath and glared at Red Harman, who had the grace to look shame-faced.

'I don't know what got into me, Steve,' he said. 'It's just that they're every one Yankees, an' while they've won the war, that don't give 'em the right to make a good Confederate eat crow in his own backyard.'

'I've been five years at war, and never seen a blamed Yankee,' growled Steve. 'So how do you know a Yankee?'

'I spent plenty of years trapping in Montana, Nebraska and Idaho,' replied Harman, and then as Steve's remark stayed with him, 'How come you've been at war and never saw a Yankee?'

Steve rubbed his face lugubriously, then grinned. 'The first four months I was at Austin getting trained as a soldier, then I got ram-rodded into a rodeo show put on for the troops. I guess I did too well, and I got made up Lieutenant and sent down to the Neuces River to round up steers for shipping out of Corpus Christi for the Mississippi to feed the

11

army. The only change I got was breaking and herding mustangs for the cavalry. I didn't get to fighting Yankees but I had my fill of Apaches and Comanches.' Red Harman's face registered interest, so Steve continued. 'Mind, the Comanches leave me alone now, they treat me like a blood brother. About a year ago I was riding point of a thousand-head herd, making for Corpus Christi, when I came upon an Indian dragging himself along the ground, making for the cover of a hill. He'd broken a leg and had a bullet wound in the arm. Well, I got a wagon to him, set his leg and took out the bullet.'

Red Harman looked at Steve incredulously. 'Why in Hades go to that trouble for an Injun? You're lucky he didn't put a knife in your back before he left.'

Steve shook his head. 'No, he tried getting away once, and I had to reset his leg, but he stayed in that wagon during three trips up the Neuces and I found him mighty good company. He got to speaking our lingo pretty good and I got to speaking Comanche. Well, I set him up with a couple of mustangs and stores just about where I found him. The last three times I rounded up a herd he was near the skyline heading a war party, and the last time I was collecting a drive for myself to ship from Mustang Island, he came on down. We palavered a long time. He told me he was Sequoia, son

12

of Bald Eagle, and he gave me two eagle feathers to wear crossed in the front of my hat, so that no matter what, no Plains Indians would cause me or mine harm. I warned him the war between the Whites was over and they may step up fighting Indians. He told me he wouldn't mind me fighting Indians so long as they were all Apaches.'

Red Harman nodded, but the doubt still showed in his eyes. He liked his Indians dead. He passed the bottle of bourbon to Steve and looked towards the corpse of T.S. Shafter without enthusiasm. 'You set yourself with that, Steve, and I'll see about getting the body over to Loomey's funeral parlour.'

Steve took the bottle to a table as far away as possible from the dead man, and rolling himself a cigarette, let himself relax and mulled over what to do with his time. Harman sent one oldster to fetch the mortician and another to tell the Marshal what happened.

When Loomey came into the saloon he glanced towards Steve and gave only a perfunctory nod in reply to Steve's greeting, and the younger man grinned to himself. It was a well-known fact long before Steve left for the army, that Loomey never really looked at a face, but his first quick appraising glance told him the least possible footage of pinewood it would take to give the recipient a close but comfortable fit for interment.

Sam Blake's welcome more than made up for Loomey's abstraction. He spared no more than a glance for Shafter's body as he made his beaming way over to Steve's table. Steve was on his feet to grip the Marshal's hand firmly. Blake clapped Steve's shoulder, then crossing to the bar, collected another glass to help out with Steve's bottle. He nodded towards the body. 'Old Eli told me the way of things, I'll just pick up his particulars from Loomey later, so for now I'll help you celebrate coming back from the war.'

'We were sorry to hear about your pa,' Blake said after a lull in the conversation. 'He'd got to full Colonel before he got killed, too.'

'Yeah.' Steve nodded, his face clouding as he realised again he would never have the pleasure of his father's rumbustious company. 'He got killed at Shiloh early on. He wrote me just before that to let me know Max Turner would keep an eye on the ranch-house, and he had fixed for a new manager called Rankin to take over the store because old Elija Ross had died.'

Blake took a deep drink of bourbon before replying. 'Rankin's a decent enough feller, but I doubt whether he's doing enough trade to do any better than cover his wages. Nobody's buying much these days. He was telling me a few days ago that his daughter intends to move in with him from Wichita.'

14

'Huh. Well, that rules out me staying above the store. Guess I'll book in at the hotel, and cool my heels around town awhile.'

'What's wrong with the ranch-house? Turner's looked after it good. Even had it painted. Last time I passed that way it looked as good as new. Plenty of cattle hogging your range too.'

'No, Sam. I don't feel ready to settle down to running a ranch yet, and anyway, I fancy getting together with some like-minded hombres and running a large herd up to Topeka for the big pay-off.'

'I'll help Turner keep an eye on the ranch-house.' The Marshal spoke soberly. 'Maybe when you've run a herd to Topeka you'll think more kindly about settling down.'

Steve spent the next two days riding out to Max Turner's Circle Star ranch and a couple of neighbouring ranches, Dan Wellard's Timberwolf and Abe Smallen's Two Dice, but he was unable to stir up any enthusiasm for a cattle drive to the railhead at Topeka. They were all decided to hang out another year for cattle prices to improve at shipside down at Galveston.

On the third morning Steve sought out Dave Rankin the store manager. At first sight he liked what he saw. Rankin was a clean-shaven, fresh-faced man in his mid-forties, with crisp, grey-flecked black hair. He stood six feet tall, but when he came around the counter to welcome Steve, he walked with a pronounced limp.

'I guess I'd know who you were without telling, Mr Grant,' Rankin said as they shook hands. 'You're the spitting image of the Colonel.'

'The name's Steve,' the younger man said with a smile. 'Yeah, I take after him in looks, but I can't say I'll ever match him in quality.'

Rankin became serious. 'Yes. He was a good man. I was very sorry when I heard he had been killed. I served alongside him before with the Rangers on the border. I was almost mended from the wound that broke my leg when he heard your old manager Elija Ross was dying, so he sent me to take his place.'

'I take it you'll be staying now that the war is over?' Steve asked.

Rankin took time answering, his face troubled. 'That depends on what you want, Steve,' he said quietly. 'Things are mighty bad, the store is only just covering the cost of keeping going. That includes my wages of course. I guess there's always a living in it for one, but very little else until the ranchers hereabouts do a whole lot better. So, now you're back, the living is yours.'

Steve shook his head slowly. 'Nope, I'll not take over, Mr Rankin. You're the manager and that's the way it stands. When prosperity turns up again I'll take my profits and you'll get your share of them.'

A smile chased away the worry lines from Rankin's face. 'Well, thanks Steve. I guess that takes care of my problems. I can send to Wichita for my daughter to move down now. Ever since I came here she's been writing, asking to join me.'

Steve nodded, and was about to make his way out of the store when the door opened and in walked Tim McCord and the two men who had sat with him a couple of days ago at the Longhorn Saloon. McCord's piercing, black eyes took in Steve, and after a nod of recognition he transferred his attention to Rankin.

'I want to buy your stock of ammunition, forty-fives, forty-threes and thirty-eights.' McCord allowed his request to hang in the air, waiting for Rankin to jump to it, but as Rankin made to move behind the counter Steve spoke.

'You're plumb out of luck, Mr McCord. We just stopped selling ammunition.'

Rankin stopped in his tracks and gave Steve a surprised look, but McCord and his two henchmen eyed the younger man with cold hostility. 'I was talking to the storeman, Grant. So let's keep it that way, then nobody'll get hurt.'

Steve's cool look took in the three men. McCord, masterful, despotic, the other two vengeful and angry. 'I happen to own this store, Mr McCord, and all we have in stock is just enough for my requirements and maybe a few friends. Anyway, we're not selling you any.'

'That's your privilege, Mister,' the slim, sardonic henchman said quietly. 'But what's to stop us taking what we need?'

'The three of you stand a fair chance of dying if you try,' replied Steve. 'Two of you will for certain. So if the odds interest you, just go ahead.'

McCord turned to look at his men, a warning in his eyes. 'As you said, Mordant, it is Grant's privilege.' He then turned his black eyes onto Steve. 'Maybe Grant, we'll never meet again, so what's passed won't matter a hill of beans, but should you ever cross me on something that matters, you'll find those guns of yours aren't fast enough.'

Steve looked unimpressed as the three men made their way out of the store; he shrugged apologetically to Rankin. 'Sorry to have spoiled a sale for you, but I reckon they're Yankees, and the less ammunition they get until they hit their own territory the better. Well, you can take it I won't interfere again. I'll be over at the Longhorn if you'd like to join me after you finish.'

'I'll be glad to,' Dave Rankin answered, and as he watched his young boss walk out of the store with the same air that had personified his father, the Colonel, a smile of contentment spread over Rankin's features. There was enough here in the store for him and his daughter, and when the good times came back, their wellbeing would be assured.

TWO

It was the fourth day and Steve Grant eyed his glass of bourbon sourly. Inactivity irked him, and drinking alone had no savour. He decided to head north and see what turned up. He had a few thousand Republican dollars to ease the way, but the money would be poor company crossing the plains and deserts.

He was debating whether or not to start on another bottle when the batwing doors swung open and three men burst into the saloon. Steve turned in his seat, then stood up and held out welcoming arms to the young men who bore down upon him with smiles spread across their faces. He did not notice the tall Negro who followed them in, to sit at the chair nearest the door.

'Steve Grant!' Jimmy Cass exclaimed delightedly. 'Heck, it's good to see you! When did you get back?'

Li Morrow and Carl Masson thumped his

19

back and punched him playfully as Steve shook their hands in turn.

'Just a few days ago,' Steve replied. 'And it's been so darned quiet I was about to go riding into the blue. It's taken me the best part of a couple of months to get back here after I finished my service, but I was doing myself some good. Where in heck have you fellers been?'

'We set ourselves a chore, Steve,' Carl Masson said quietly. 'We had some investigating to do and Li had some doctoring to do on old Amos.' Masson nodded towards the door where the Negro sat.

Steve looked across to the black man and back to the tall, fair-haired, husky, Stageline owner's son. 'I'll get the drinks in,' he said, 'And maybe you'll tell me all about it.' He moved to the bar, but they all crowded after him to shake hands and exchange greetings with Red Harman, whose face widened into a grin of pleasure.

At length they took bottles and glasses to the table next to Amos, and Red Harman brought the coloured man a foaming glass of beer. Li Morrow introduced Steve Grant to the older man who greeted Steve in well modulated, dignified tones. 'I'm pleased to make your acquaintance, Mr Grant. It's a pleasure to meet any friend of these young gentlemen.'

'That goes for me too, Amos,' Steve

replied seriously. 'Welcome to Waco.'

'He's not staying long, Steve, any more than we are,' Jimmy Cass remarked as he poured out generous measures for them all.

Steve looked at his friends in some surprise. Their faces had taken on a seriousness that seemed to mean a common cause, and somehow he sensed that Amos was part of that cause. He studied them anew. Cass, a well-built six-footer, fresh of face and cheerful. Morrow, dark, swarthy, of medium height, a qualified doctor and son of the Waco banker, and Masson, his face now set into hard lines. Steve sipped his drink and waited for them to expound. When they did not, he felt he should press the point; if anything mattered enough to set them riding away to right it, then he wanted to be alongside them.

'Look, you fellers! If you've got any reason for riding out of Waco, suppose you tell me about it. Four guns are better than three.'

His companions looked at one another and after a long spell they each nodded agreement. Morrow and Masson indicated that Jimmy Cass should pass their story.

'I guess that war's pretty ugly no matter how high-minded the contestants are,' Cass said at length. 'But there are limits beyond which no man should go. However, there've been Yankees who did things that war cannot excuse. You may not have come across many of them, Steve, having spent your time down on the Neuces. We heard you'd been posted there when we arrived at Austin, so maybe you've never heard of Sheridan's Light Horse?'

Steve shook his head. 'Nope. All my fighting was against the Apache and Comanches.'

'Yeah,' Cass murmured. 'Well, we had heard about Sheridan's Light Horse, but we never knew if what we heard was truth or tall stories. That is, until the war ended.' He paused, the picture in his mind making him grimace with hate. 'For a couple of years we had known a fine family, the Billons, who lived just north of Wayneboro. They made us welcome at any time we could get leave and any other time we were in the neighbourhood. There were five girls and three boys, and we were especially fond of Bella, Dianne and Griselda Billon, enough to keep us visiting, and enough to set us hot-foot for Wayneboro at the end of the war.'

Jimmy Cass paused, searching for the poise to allow him to continue the story without emotion. 'Well we found the house no more than a mass of rubble, everything destroyed. Amos was the only living creature left, and he was living in a toolshed, the only building that survived the fire. Sheridan's Light Horse had paid a visit, and they had stripped the house of everything valuable, loading things into covered wagons. They killed Mr Billon and the young Billon boys, all the man-servants except for Amos, who they left for dead. Then the girls and female servants had been used by ninety odd soldiers. One girl of nine died and Mrs Billon was used as were the girls. Finally they had been hustled away into carriages and sent towards Wayneboro. Our own cannon fire hit them just outside Wayneboro and they were all killed. Amos found them and buried them at the side of the road. We found that Sheridan's Light Horse had treated more than a hundred homes the same way, so we swore we'd track down Sheridan's Light Horse and salivate every last one.'

'That's going to be a tall order,' Steve interposed. 'With the war over, that outfit must have split up and headed in all directions. It'll take you a lifetime to round that lot up.'

Jimmy Cass shook his head. 'No. There's only thirty-odd men left of Sheridan's Light Horse. We had to get Amos to hospital where Li could fix his leg properly and see to the face cuts he'd collected, so Carl and I made the rounds of hospitals trying to trace anyone who'd ridden with the scallywags. Well, we visited a lot of hospitals but at last it paid off down in Brunswick, Georgia.'

'How come?' Steve asked, his interest alive.

'We found a man who I reckon was only hanging onto life so that he could get someone interested enough to wipe out the survivors of Sheridan's Light Horse, and

23

particularly the Major who commanded them. His name was Rain, one of three lieutenants under the Major's orders. He admitted all the things they did, pillaging, plundering and rape. Most of the goods and valuables they took from the houses were sent to some place north of Harrisburg, Pennsylvania, where Sheridan owned the property. Everything was to be sold to help finance the war. The rest and best of the goods were stored in the Major's hideaway, and when they had five or six wagon loads, one squad trekked them to Nebraska to store on the Major's property.

Jimmy Cass paused, taking a long drink before continuing. 'The intention had been to share everything cached in Nebraska between them all, about one hundred men all told, but with the war getting near to its end, the Major had said it was time to take up a more positive line; and so, two squads were given offensive roles where the fighting was bloodiest, and chances of survival slimmest. The two squads were thrust into the fore-front, and Lieutenant Rain was of the opin-ion that he was the sole survivor of the sixty men who he believed had been sacrificed by Major McCord to cut the shares of the stolen booty. The lieutenant seemed in no way sorry about the way he'd fought his war, but at losing his share, and there was no way he could collect. He was short of two legs and an arm, and a couple of days after he had described McCord and his men, he died from gangrene. So between what he told us and what Amos remembers of them, we'll find them, given time. We know they headed west, and we found a few places where they'd stopped, like Meridian, Monroe, Shreveport and Dallas.'

'You say McCord?' Steve asked, excitement rising in him.

'Yeah. Major Tim McCord,' Jimmy Cass and Carl Masson answered in unison. 'Why!?'

Steve told them about his brush with the man calling himself McCord a few days ago and again yesterday morning. His friends sat bolt upright in their chairs, drinking in every word.

'They were Yankees, that's for sure,' Steve added. 'About twenty-two of 'em, and McCord was most certainly the boss man. A word from him and they did as he said, pronto.'

'Well. What are we going to do about it?' Carl Masson asked. 'Are we going after them?'

'What! Four of us, riding in with guns blazing just like that?' Steve grunted. 'I saw twenty-odd. There were maybe ten more looking after a remuda and stock somewhere out of town.' He shook his head. 'That's not the way, Carl. Take time. We're not going to lose them now. According to the story the dying man told you, they've got a powerful reason for heading towards Nebraska. Let's trail them. Pick them off where we can, a couple at a time in saloons or anywhere we can pick a quarrel with a few of them, so by the time they get to Nebraska we'll have whittled them down to manageable numbers. If they've got a fortune waiting at the end of the journey, the men remaining alive will be more concerned counting out their new shares rather than being hell-bent upon revenging them.'

Li Morrow's face split into a delightful smile. Cass and Masson seeing his approval, nodded.

'You haven't lost any of your guile, Steve,' Li Morrow said quietly. 'You always were the cagiest hombre I've known, and for one, I'm sure glad you want to take sides with us.'

'Well then,' Steve said as he stood up, 'Don't let's rush into things. You all need to see your folks, spend some time with them and get geared up for a long trail. I'll go and scout around. If they've already moved away I'll trail them a bit to make sure of the way they're heading.'

'Yeah, you're right, Steve,' Carl Masson said. 'We're not going to lose them now, so what say we set off in four days from now?'

Steve nodded his agreement, and the others drained their glasses and stood up, ready to go their separate ways. Amos laid his hand on Steve's arm and looked at him earnestly.

'Just don't go killing all of those polecats, Mr Grant. Some of them belong to me.'

'Yes, Amos.' Steve was equally serious. 'I'm sure they do.'

The friends separated, Steve to saddle up and go looking for signs, the others to seek out their folks. Amos went with Li Morrow. Red Harman waved them a cheery farewell from the bar.

Seth Dyer, the livery-man, eyed the deep-chested bay mustang as Steve Grant saddled up, his rheumy eyes appreciating the good points of the young stallion. 'That's as fine a hunk of horse-flesh I've seen all the years I've handled horses,' Dyer remarked as Steve pulled a cinch tight. 'And that's getting close to seventy years now.'

Steve turned to smile at the oldster who had always found time to pass a kindly word to children and young adults, and was well known in the territory for honest trading. 'Glad you think so, Seth. I reckoned he was something special when I saw him down at the head of the Neuces. Your opinion is better than most, but I don't think you've handled horses as long as you say, you don't look a day over forty.'

'Can't say I feel much more than forty,'

Seth replied with a grin. 'But seventy it is. If you ever get thoughts of running a horse-ranch, then that's the one to start with. Given good mares I'd say he'd breed true to his likeness every time.'

Steve backed the animal out of its stall, and both men appraised the mustang critically. 'Yeah, you could be right, Seth, and one of these days I might just do as you say.'

Steve led the horse outside and rode towards the bank of the Brazos, then made his way beside the slow-running river for a few miles. For most of the year the Brazos remained placid, but when the rains came, and the water drained from the plateau to the west of Waco, the river became a raging torrent that spilled over its mile-wide banks here and there, catching the unwary rancher.

Bunches of sleek, well-fed longhorns moved bad-temperedly out of his way. He noticed that no more than half of them carried a brand, and they were mostly Cass's Halfmoon. He decided that if and when he and his pards had brought McCord's men to their proper retribution, he would find enough help to drive a large herd of cattle to the Topeka rail-head.

It did not take exceptional scouting ability for Steve to pick up the signs he sought. Careful attention to detail brought him to the opinion that five wagons had been hauled by teams of four horses, and one wagon, obviously very heavy, drawn by six horses. He concluded there were also about twenty ridden horses and a large remuda of spare horses.

An hour later he found where they had camped, just six miles west of Waco. Grass was broken down where the wagons had formed a tight circle and a newly-picked skeleton of a steer lay just outside the perimeter, where it had obviously been butchered to provide McCord's men with prime steaks.

He followed the trail they had left after breaking camp for about fifteen miles, always heading north, then he turned west to gain height up the steady gradient to the plateau. From the escarpment he had a good view of the lowland between the bottom of the slopes and the sluggish river. He was able to follow its course for about ten miles in each direction, and to the north he detected moving specks that he deduced was the remainder of Sheridan's Light Horse.

Steve sat easy in the saddle, stroking his mount's neck and talking aloud to the animal. 'Well, Apache, old son, I guess that'll do for now. We know where they are and where they're going.'

He was about to turn the horse around when he saw a rider hugging the river bank about five miles away. There seemed to be an urgency about the man and Steve rolled himself a smoke, keeping the rider in view. Every now and again the rider was lost to Steve's view as the rolling terrain hid him, but each time he came in sight again; he held the direction, and Steve concluded the man was heading for Zeke Dale's ranch.

Instinctively, Steve set Apache to the slope, picking his way to keep himself out of sight of the other rider. He knew the small ranch below belonged to Zeke Dale who managed the place for most of the year with the help of his wife Josie and the son who could only be about sixteen years old now. He remembered when Red Harman gave him some details of men who had returned from the war with wounds, that Zeke had lost an arm. He also remembered Josie Dale and her dark-haired beauty. The hardship of her life had only enhanced her vivacity and radiant good looks. If Sheridan's Light Horse had passed that way it would be feasible that at least one of their number would take a chance at taking his pleasure the way he had during the war.

Steve arrived at the windbreak as the other rider drew up in front of the ranch-house. He dismounted and ground-hitched his mount, made his way quickly through the belt of trees to the inner edge.

Zeke and his son Dan were busy cutting and stacking wood into a small outbuilding. They both straightened up as the rider dismounted, and made their way to greet him. At the same time Josie Dale opened the ranch-house door and stood framed in the doorway. Even at the distance, Steve saw she was still as beautiful as he remembered. He also noticed that Zeke had lost his right arm, and now only carried a gun on the left hip.

The newcomer, a big, thickset man, with close-cut beard, spared hardly a look for the menfolk and gave his attention to Josie. 'Howdye Ma'am,' he drawled. 'I caught sight of you-all a while back when we passed this way, and I came to thinking you're missing out on things. A pretty woman like you needs something better than a half-man, so I've called to make things up to you.'

A look of cold fury settled on Josie's face, and Zeke started to lumber forward. The boy was quicker however, and he threw himself at the interloper.

The man stepped aside and gave Dan a savage blow as he slid past, sending the lad hurtling into the bottom step of the veran-dah stairway. Zeke slipped off balance in his eagerness to reach for his gun and spread-eagled himself just a couple of feet away from the man who grinned evilly as Zeke's gun bounced at his feet. Slowly the man reached for his gun and drew it carelessly, one eye on Josie's shocked face.

'Your worries are over, ma'am,' he said calmly. 'I'll ventilate 'em both then I'll come

31

in and join you.'

Josie screamed in unadulterated horror as the man deliberately aimed his gun at Zeke, who was scrambling to his feet, his face contorted with rage. There was a shot, and Josie screamed again, turning her face away, unable to look at her husband and son. She waited for the second shot, with sobs welling up from deep within her; but it failed to happen, and she opened her eyes, ready to throw herself upon the man in an effort to save her son. The tableau presented before her was to remain with her for always, and she never ceased to thank the providence that had brought Steve Grant to her neck of the woods.

Zeke was gaining his feet, Dan was rubbing his neck at the foot of the stairs, the interloper was stretched out inert, with blood seeping from the side of his head, and Steve Grant was walking across the paddock from the windbreak.

'Oh. Thank God!' Josie cried, running down the steps into the protective arm of her husband. He held her tight for a moment then they turned to welcome Steve, and Dan pulled himself off the ground to give Steve a relieved smile of welcome.

Zeke took his arm from around Josie's shoulder and grasped Steve's outstretched palm tightly. He looked a bit shame-faced at being unable to sort out his own troubles, then grinned a trifle ruefully. 'Well, Steve, I always reckoned I'd welcome seeing you back,' he said. 'But I never guessed you'd be this welcome.'

Josie and Dan closed in to shake the newcomer's hand, and Steve could see the shock had rattled Josie considerably. He hardly spared a glance at the prone figure and headed them towards the ranch-house steps.

'I'm sure glad I happened along,' he said. 'Although I had the hombre in my sights for a considerable time. Only when I saw the way he was heading I reckoned he'd take closer watching.'

They entered the neat, shining interior of the ranch and Steve, with alacrity, accepted Josie's invitation to a cup of coffee.

'That galoot is one of a pack of Union men making their way back up north, and there's not one of them fit to live among decent folk. They must have passed along the river a couple of hours ago. I expect this one caught sight of the ranch-house.'

'How come you had him in your sight?' Zeke asked.

'I just wanted to be sure the way they were headed. We'll be trailing them in earnest in a few days. That gang has got a lot to answer for.' Steve went on to recount quickly what his three pards had told him about Sheridan's Light Horse, and his listeners were horrified.

Steve had a couple of cups of coffee then stood up ready to leave. He turned to young Dan. 'Perhaps you'll give me some help to tie the corpse over his saddle. I intend taking him to his boss-man.'

'Oh, sure thing, Steve,' Dan agreed, and he followed Steve outside quickly. Zeke's face looked troubled.

'You say you're taking the corpse to his pards, Steve?'

Steve looked up as he turned the corpse over and started digging into the dead man's pockets, and nodded. 'You're taking that chance so that they won't come here looking for him. Isn't that so?' Zeke persisted.

'No. I'm just keeping things tidy, Zeke,' Steve replied. 'They wouldn't come looking anyway, because one less means a better share each of what's waiting for 'em somewhere in Nebraska. I'm betting they'll leave me alone, they're not set on any devilry yet. The odd one, like this coyote, was just acting out of line. The last one that acted the same way I salivated a few days ago in town.'

Steve's search of the dead man's pockets brought to light tobacco, papers, about twenty gold coins and a disc on the end of a tag proving him to be Union Soldier, S.C. Udell. No. 16374. He showed the disc to Zeke, then replaced it. Five of the gold coins he replaced, the others he handed to Josie.

'He's not going to have any use for these,

and I reckon you've a right to 'em.' Steve unhitched the dead man's gunbelt and reached for the gun that lay near him, replacing it in its holster. He handed the belt and guns to Dan. 'Your pa will show you how to handle these and tell you the only time to use 'em.'

Together Steve and Dan manhandled Udell's body onto his mount, then Steve took hold of the lead rein. Josie stepped forward and laid a hand on his arm.

'Thank you, Steve. God must have guided you here today. Take care and look in on your way back so that we'll know you're all right.'

Steve's smile was reassuring and he nodded as he led the horse towards the windbreak. 'I sure will, and quit worrying.'

He passed through the windbreak until he came to Apache, which nickered gently at his approach. Tying the lead rein of Udell's horse to his saddle cantle, he mounted and eased out of the trees to head north.

THREE

Tim McCord and Mordant rode in easy relaxed manner, keeping a couple of hundred yards ahead of the chuck-wagon. Bunches of cattle bellowed and grumbled their way out of the line of progress, then regrouped to eye the passing wagons and riders malevolently.

Mordant eyed the sleek cattle, and in his greedy way saw them only as dollars on the hoof. 'At the speed we're making, Major, we could just as well be herding a few thousand head of beeves.'

McCord looked across at his lieutenant frostily. He shook his head decisively. 'Nope! There's a heck of a lot of territory between here and Topeka, and a lot of it where a couple of thousand head of cattle would churn up enough dust to choke a man, and there's always something turning up to spook them into running every which way like mindless demons.' He shook his head again. 'No, we'll ride trouble-free until we get up into Oklahoma, then we'll collect a couple of big herds from some worn-out cowpokes who've nursed 'em nigh on a thousand miles.'

Mordant thought about it a bit. 'Taking over a couple of herds could cause us grief, we could lose a lot of men.'

This time McCord's lips parted in a cold smile. 'So long as you, Hook and I keep our heads down, I couldn't care if the rest of the outfit came to grief. You think about it, Mordant. If we drove a herd from here, every last man would be there at Nebraska, demanding his share, and talking his head off. By battling for the beef up in the Badlands we could lose most of them, the others we could handle.' McCord paused for a minute so that Mordant's greedy nature could adjust. 'Anyway, only the three of us have the style to live the way such money allows.'

Mordant's quick laugh told McCord that his lieutenant agreed with him all down the line, and McCord was content. There was prize enough for three, and Hook and Mordant would do all his legwork for him.

They reached a humped hill, and stayed close to it while it kept in line with the river. Then, out of a break in the hill, Steve Grant appeared, toting the cadaver on the led horse. Steve sat his mount calmly, waiting for the two men to react. Both men pulled in their mounts and eyed Steve without any visible degree of concern. Neither man evinced any interest in the corpse.

Steve indicated the dead man behind him. 'The cadaver's name is Udell.'

'How come he's a cadaver?' McCord asked quietly.

'I came across him at a small ranch-house that you passed a couple of hours ago. There's a pretty woman keeping the place going with a husband who lost an arm fighting against you hombres, and a young son. Seems Udell fancied his chances, and when I arrived he had poleaxed the youngster, and he was about to salivate the husband who was on the ground. I thought you'd want him back so you could give him a Yankee burial.'

As he spoke, Steve reached behind him and unhitched the lead rein of the dead man's horse from his cantle, then when the two men said nothing he continued. 'I gave Udell's belt and guns to the youngster, so he can learn to take care of any other trash that shows up on his porch.'

McCord and Mordant showed nothing of their thoughts as they considered the Texan. McCord was however weighing up the chances of gunning down the level-eyed young man who showed him no respect whatever. Such was his confidence that the possible aftermath of his victory deterred him. The rancher would have known Steve's intention to return the dead man and if Steve failed to show up, then a hornets' nest could be stirred up in Waco that could set the couple of Forts that lay ahead to look out for his party. He wanted no trouble this side of the Badlands, so he allowed a smile to appear briefly on his lips.

The chuck-wagon rounded the hill into view when McCord spoke. 'We'll take him off your hands, Grant. He never did have any sense. I'm mighty pleased your business at the ranch-house got you there at the right time. Maybe you'll pass on my regrets when you get back.'

Steve nodded briefly, then swung his

mount around and rode into the break in the hill. From the top of the hill he saw the remuda and wagons below as they streamed past. Just two riders stayed behind with spades to bury the dead man. One wagon, drawn by six horses, was about twice as long as the others, and the canvas cover was tightly drawn under both ends and sides. He felt he would like to see what was being carried in the wagon but decided that now was not a good time, and headed back towards the Dales' ranch.

Almost one hundred miles north of Fort Worth, the riders atop Dunn's Peak watched Sheridan's Light Horse ford the Red River. The township of Matson lay ahead, and the watchers were not surprised to see the wagons take up a defensive circle formation.

'I guess they've worked up enough of a thirst to send most of them into town,' Jimmy Cass remarked. 'What do we do, Steve? Let them celebrate first or hit the town before them?'

'Let's see how many of them make for town,' he replied. 'If there's only a handful left we may be able to take a look into their wagons, and with a bit of luck haze away their remuda.'

Carl Masson nodded his agreement and Amos smiled his content. Amos had filled out and now looked as durable as a Canadian

Redwood. He packed a Colt on his right hip and spent his spare time grabbing for it and aiming. He would never be greased lightning but he intended to exact revenge for the fate of his beloved Billon family. He pointed to a little arroyo. 'I'll go and get a meal ready now, so we'll be ready whenever you want, Mr Grant,' he said.

Steve smiled his agreement and when the Negro made his way to the arroyo, the others stretched out and watched McCord's men milling around the camp. The remuda they noticed, was staked out downwind, between the camp and the river.

An hour later Steve and Li Morrow slid alongside the prone figures of Carl Masson and Jimmy Cass who had stayed on watch while they ate. Jimmy Cass pointed to a moving dust pall a few miles away from Matson.

'There they go,' he said laconically. 'Twenty-six we counted.'

'Yeah, and we can only make out seven still in camp,' Masson added. He pointed. 'Two hombres looking after the remuda, two more making the rounds of the wagons and three more around the fire.'

Steve and Morrow stared through the fading daylight and were just able to pick out the guards.

'Looks like seven is right,' Steve agreed. 'Well, after you have got yourselves outside some chow we'll see what troubles we can think up for them.'

Later, the five men packed their gear and tied everything down on their mounts, then with Steve taking the lead, they set out for the ford and the camp beyond. When they gained the north bank of the Red River, they stopped to consider their moves. Steve immediately came to the point, speaking in a low voice.

'There are seven of them and five of us, so from an even start they've got the odds. I don't think it's in our nature to gun them down cold, but they don't deserve any better. If any one of you think they should have a chance, then we'll give 'em that chance.'

'I say we salivate 'em,' Jimmy Cass growled without hesitation.

'That goes for me too,' Masson said. 'Don't forget there's another twenty-six of them, we can't afford to take chances with these.'

'My job is to save life,' Li Morrow put in. 'But I believe I'll be saving lives along the way by killing these monsters.'

'They didn't give the Billons any chances,' Amos said with finality.

'Right then,' Steve whispered. 'We'll skirt around them about a quarter of a mile. Amos will stay with the horses, and we'll come back on foot. You, Carl, and Jimmy will take the guard on the remuda and Li, you'll help me with the guard patrolling the other side of the camp and the others around the fire. They

41

may have changed turns, but I expect the pattern will be the same, and when I reckon we're ready I'll give three owl-hoots.'

They skirted the ring of wagons in a wide loop until they came to a break in a low hill. In the lee of the steeper side they dismounted and gave the horses over to Amos' care.

'When the shooting dies down, Amos, give us at least half-an-hour before you come looking for us,' Steve warned the older man, then the four friends set off for the camp.

When they came in sight of the camp-fire things had changed. There were now six men seated close to it, playing cards, and one man was passing between two wagons heading for the remuda, so they waited, giving him time to take up his duty.

'I'll take him,' Carl Masson said drily. 'Then I'll join you behind the wagons, Jimmy.'

'Wait!' Li Morrow broke in with a sibilant whisper. 'No point in making a noise killing that hombre, you'd best leave him to me. You just carry on, don't wait for any sign from me.'

Steve did not argue. Doctor and life-saver Morrow may be, but certainly no-one Steve had known threw a knife with such deadly accuracy. So Li moved away into the darkness and the other three pointed out to each other just where they would place themselves, and satisfied, they parted company.

Taking his place beside the long wagon he had noticed before the affair at Dales' ranch, Steve eyed the six men beside the fire. The flames licking up from the newly-placed brushwood showed them for what they were; big, hard-necked ruffians, callousness in every line of their features. There were four card players, the other two sat on upturned boxes, drinking coffee.

He allowed a few more minutes to slide away, all the time trying to fight against his inborn reluctance to gun men down without warning. As he drew his six-guns he emitted three owl-hoots.

Any squeamishness Steve might have felt proved unnecessary. The owl-hoots galvanized the men around the fire into action. They flung themselves out of the firelight, clawing at their guns at the same time.

The card-players made it to the ground fit to fight, but Steve's guns claimed the other two men before they could fire the guns that appeared in their hands with creditable speed. He rolled away along the side of the wagon as guns roared and bullets thudded into the ground where he had lain. Then Cass and Masson opened up, aiming for the gun flashes, and a man screamed as one of the bullets found a mark.

'How do you like it, you Yankee murderers?' Jimmy Cass' voice carried above the gunfire.

The Yankees made no reply and the three men remaining alive held their fire. Two tried rolling towards the cover of the wagons so that they might escape in the darkness and the other rolled towards an object under a canvas cover which stood just out of the range of the firelight.

Steve held his fire, straining his sight to locate the men, but Jimmy Cass and Carl Masson kept up their fire. A couple of minutes passed by when it seemed the pardners were holding down the Yankees, then the balance changed. From the centre of the camp came a stuttering rat-a-tat of explosions and something new to Steve Grant sent steel winging towards his pards. Flame gouted from the quick-firing instrument and above the noise, Steve heard the quick cry of pain from one of his friends.

Anger sent Steve crawling under the wagon to get near to the man who was causing so much havoc. He saw the bent figures of the other two Yankees, who, heartened by the advantage their confederate had gained, were running to help, and he sent them ploughing to the ground with two seemingly unaimed shots, then as the tongues of flame swept in an arc towards him Steve kept hopping around sideways to keep ahead of the chattering gun.

He was close enough now to see the gun, and the humped figure of the man behind it, and when the arcing muzzle had almost reached him Steve jumped, clearing the gun and landing feet-first against the man's chest. They both rolled over a couple of times, the man grabbing his side-arms as he went, and Steve was only a split-second faster in firing.

Slowly, Steve got to his feet, and as he heard the sounds of horses being driven into the night he called out to his pards.

'Hold your fire. I'm coming over. It's all done.'

Carl Masson answered, and his voice seemed strained.

'C'mon, Steve. Seems you were luckier than us.'

Masson's words had Steve crawling quickly under the wagon behind which Masson and Cass had lain. He found them sitting up with blood seeping out of wounds. Cass was wounded in the upper right arm and Masson's chest seemed covered with blood.

'How bad is it?' he asked, his question including them both, then specifically to Masson, 'You going to be able to fork a cayuse?'

'Yeah, I guess so,' Masson replied. 'I think it's no worse than a chunk of flesh and muscle out of my chest underneath the armpit, and maybe it nicked a rib.'

Conjecture was unnecessary because they were joined by Li Morrow who confirmed Carl Masson's own diagnosis and stated that

Jimmy Cass had a broken humerus in addition to a large slice of muscle out of his right arm.

'I'll get the cayuses,' Steve said as Li used handkerchiefs to staunch the blood flowing from his pards. 'You'd all best think of heading back to Waco.'

Twenty minutes later Steve and Amos brought the horses, and Li Morrow soon had his medical kit unpacked to attend to the sterilisation and dressing of his friends' wounds, then the three fit men helped Cass and Masson into their saddles.

'Well, Li, you're the doctor. What do we do?' Steve asked.

'We've got to go back, Steve. They'll last our riding steadily, but they'll take careful minding to get as good as new.'

'In that case I'll keep you company for a day,' Steve said. 'After that I'll keep these hombres in sight and bring 'em what grief I can on the way.'

'To heck with that, Steve!' Jimmy Cass burst out. 'Why saddle yourself with our quarrel on your lonesome? Anyway! What can you hope to do against twenty-six of them?'

'Huh. It's a long way to Nebraska, I could get all sorts of luck before they get there. But I'll just keep tabs on them, so that you'll know where to look when you're fit and ready.'

'I'd like to ride with you, Mr Grant, if you'll have me,' Amos put in quietly. 'Now I've seen them again I never want to lose sight of them until the last one is dead.'

Steve looked at the other three in the fading firelight, and one after another they nodded. He turned back to Amos and smiled. 'I'll be glad to have your company, Amos,' he replied warmly.

FOUR

Tim McCord hauled his mount to a halt and held his arm aloft to bring his followers to a stop. The moon was now well up and the light was sufficient to bring immediate reaction to McCord's signal.

'Something's wrong!' McCord snapped, pointing to the shadowy circle of wagons in the distance. 'The fire's out, so they've either had trouble or they're expecting it.'

'Had it I reckon,' replied Mordant. 'Otherwise the fire would have been kept in to make things look normal.'

'Yeah. You'd better take half-a-dozen men in to check on things.'

A sardonic smile played on Mordant's lips as he selected a few men for the chore. He was used to being first whenever an element of risk came up. The dangers never bothered him, but his greedy soul would not permit him to take chances for someone else's gain, and he had long since consoled himself that when settling day came, he would do the settling and take all.

The small group of riders stayed in a tight bunch until they were just outside accurate six-gun range, then Mordant halted them and told them to dismount. 'Right then, we'll walk the broncs in a closing circle of the wagons, using them as shields until we know exactly what's waiting. Tie the lead reins to cantles.' Then with Mordant in the lead, they played follow-my-leader around the camp, inexorably closing in, and always keeping horseflesh between them and possibly flying lead.

They soon discovered the remuda was missing, and that Joplin was dead from a knife wound, so they closed in upon the camp more rapidly. At a signal from Mordant, the other men dropped to the ground as he continued to lead the line of horses. Any watchers would have kept the horses in sight, and the six men who wriggled their ways to the wagons would have created the havoc of surprise. But nobody waited. In the thin light inert figures showed up, still, in the obscene postures of death.

Duke Whelan gave a low whistle as he surveyed the still figures and called out to

Mordant. 'There's nothing here except our own dead.'

Mordant arrived and took in the scene. Seven men were dead, and the remuda hazed away. Even the machine-gun hadn't saved them. He turned to Whelan. 'Go and tell the Major,' then to the others, 'Get the fire going again, Dill, and the rest of you take a look inside every wagon.'

When McCord and the others rode in, Mordant was able to tell him that nobody lurked in the wagons, nothing had been stolen, and only the dead men and the missing remuda proved the camp had been raided.

The fire started to take hold, lending some warmth to the grim picture as McCord, Mordant and Sergeant Hook checked each dead man. At length they stood a few feet away from the leaping flames to consider things.

'Well, it wasn't Injuns,' Hook said blandly. 'They'd have ruined everything they couldn't steal, and they'd have taken scalps too.'

'I'd gathered that!' McCord snapped. 'And there are only two considerations left. Either some horse traders took a fancy to our stock, or this was done because of who we are.' He paused, allowing the thoughts to sink into his henchmen's skulls, then continued, 'come sun-up I'll see if I can pick up any trail of the hombres. You, Mordant, can take eight men to find the broncs, and I'll leave you, Hook, to make sure we'll find a camp when we get back.'

At dawn McCord found to his chagrin that whatever sign may have been left behind had been trampled beyond his ability to define, and he spent a day of utter frustration looking for a trail that would lead him to revenge.

Mordant succeeded in his chore of recapturing the lost remuda, but he and his men were saddle-weary by the time every horse was back at camp under care.

Only Hook, the imperturbable, ginger giant was good-tempered when the three men drew together after their evening meal.

'Well, we're no nearer knowing who we're up against,' McCord said at length, drawing on his cheroot. 'But from here on, we've got to be wary of anyone crossing our paths, and I think from now we should press on until we get to near Wichita and steal the first good-sized herd that shows up.'

'Yeah, the sooner the better,' Mordant said laconically.

'One thing we know,' said Hook quietly, 'Is that we've been followed and watched. So when we move, we've got to have eyes a lot wider than we've had up to now.'

'McCord's quick glance at Hook showed his approval. 'Yes, exactly my own opinion, and you're just the man to take care of it.'

They broke camp and headed north, Mc-Cord dictating a faster pace than before. The dead had been buried and each man mentally wrestled with the new ratio of share-out now that their numbers had decreased by seven.

Three days had passed since Steve and Amos had parted company with Li Morrow and the wounded Cass and Masson. They had stayed one night in Matson, giving Mc-Cord time to get rolling, then they had headed north-west, climbing to the high plateau where the tall grass fed countless cattle, and innumerable small humped hills broke the tedium of endless plain.

'I suppose you know where we're going, Mr Grant,' Amos said as they stopped on the fourth day for a meal.

'Look, Amos, there's no sense in calling me Mr Grant. I'd like it better if you call me Steve. And as far as knowing where we're going, all I know is the general direction. If I can remember right from a map my father had, south-east Nebraska is dead north from here, through Oklahoma and Kansas, and we've been in Oklahoma since crossing the Red River. When we've crossed the Canadian, Cimarron and Medicine Lodge Creek we'll be in Kansas. Could be all of four months before we get back to Waco.'

Amos pushed the Stetson Li Morrow had

given him to the back of his head. 'I don't mind how long it takes, riding free like this is better than I ever believed possible. Before Mr Morrow doctored me back to health, I'd never gone further from the Billon's house and fields than Wayneboro, just a few miles down the road, in the stores cart.'

Steve stripped the gear from the horses to let them graze in comfort, while the Negro searched around for tinder. He realised that Amos was in no way complaining about his lot at the hands of the Billon family, but marvelling aloud at the seemingly endless, unspoiled terrain that beckoned one on from sunrise to sunset. Steve conceded he'd never given much thought to it before, but upon reflection, decided he was never happier than when riding towards the skyline, on the move.

Later, eating their hard tack, Steve felt that sixth sense of the plainsman niggling at him, and his unease got him to his feet, scanning every inch of territory and taking particular care with the hills. He realised that the hills, although small, could hide a thousand men who were intent upon maintaining careful surveillance, and he could only conclude that any watchers would be Indians.

In consequence, before saddling up, Steve took out from his saddle-roll the eagle feathers Sequoia had given to him and fixed them in the band of his sombrero. Amos watched him curiously. Then, once in the saddle, Steve fractionally changed direction so that they moved further and further away from the line of hills.

Steve's instincts were right, but he had wrongly diagnosed the cause. Indians there were in plenty hidden in the hills, but one man had knelt in the tall grass far to the east, viewing him and Amos through army binoculars as they ate. One relentless man who hunted with the remorseless skill of the Indian hunter, the ginger-haired giant, Caleb Hook, McCord's trusted henchman.

'So, Mister Grant. You're the one we can thank for cutting down the shareholders,' Caleb Hook mused. 'It beats me how just two men could cause so much damage. Well, we'll end your run before this day is done.' He made his slithering way through the grass down the long, steady grade to where his horse waited, then climbing into the saddle, sent the animal at a brisk pace to the south-east. Two and a half hours later he pulled his mount to a stop beside Tim Mc-Cord and Mordant. McCord glanced at the sergeant's sweating horse significantly.

'Well, I can't see anybody chasing you, Caleb,' McCord said drily. 'So I guess you've got some news.'

'I sure have, and I doubt you'll believe it.' He then deliberately took time out to roll himself a smoke. McCord curbed his impatience, he knew Hook had a sense of the dramatic. 'I caught up with the two hombres who attacked the camp, that is as near as I could see 'em, and one is an old black man.'

'Two!' Incredulity was stamped on both McCord's and Mordant's features as McCord barked the question.

'Yeah, two. And by my reckoning, we can thank the same hombre for salivating nine of our men since we arrived at Waco.'

Both men grasped the significance of Hook's remark immediately. A glance passed between McCord and Mordant almost of disbelief.

'You mean Grant. Steve Grant?' McCord asked, and Hook nodded.

'Yeah, the same. I reckon he must be something special.'

'He's something special all right!' McCord snapped. 'So special I want him dead. Take a few men, Caleb, and bring him in.'

Hook drew deeply on his cigarette, then his lips parted in a cruel grin. 'It'll be my pleasure after I've taken a meal,' he said, spurring his horse away in the direction of the rolling wagons. The other two men watched him go, then Mordant voiced his thoughts.

'I've got a gut feeling that Hook won't find it so easy to take Grant.'

McCord snorted. He reckoned he knew Hook's capabilities. 'There's no way Grant will get away now that Caleb's got the scent.'

Mordant made no reply, but he was in no way convinced.

It needed a couple of hours to sundown when Steve stopped to take a good look around before picking a spot to camp for the night. He still had Indians in mind, but the riders he glimpsed to the south-east were not Indians. They were too far away for recognition but Steve was never in doubt. The riders had him and Amos in view and they started to fan out.

'We've got company, Amos,' he shouted. 'McCord's men by the looks of it. About six of 'em. We've got to head for the hills.'

Steve pinpointed a break in the hills a couple of miles away and sent Apache racing towards it. The skewbald that Amos rode was no sluggard, so very little daylight showed between the two animals.

Now and again Steve glanced over his shoulder. Each time the riders had spread further apart but they were making no impression on the bay stallion and skewbald until disaster struck. The skewbald caught a foreleg in a gopher hole and crashed to the ground, sending Amos flying into a heap.

Amos' cry made Steve look around in dismay. He hauled Apache around and stopped alongside the horse that had now regained its feet. He felt the animal's leg, quickly deciding the skewbald had strained the limb only, then he crossed to Amos who was already sitting up. Hurriedly he dragged the bemused man to his feet, and getting back into his saddle, he hauled and shouted at Amos to get up behind him.

It seemed an age before Amos was seated, and the pursuers were nearly in range for gunplay. He sent his horse for the break, urging and entreating the animal to maintain its speed despite the double load, and the stallion made it seem easy.

Bullets were singing their way mighty close when the horse ran into the break and up the long, curving slope that narrowed about a hundred yards from the summit. At the curve stood a large outcrop, and Steve eased the animal back, guiding it behind the rock.

'Keep your head down, Amos!' he shouted as he hauled his Winchester out of the saddle-holster and dropped to the ground. Then he scaled the rock, searching out his best vantage point.

One rider came into view, his lathered mount taking the grade at speed. The man's rifle was in his hand and there was deadly purpose in every line of him, so Steve took rapid aim and fired. The rider slewed drunkenly in the saddle before slipping and hanging by one foot in the stirrup, bringing his mount to a stop. Another rider appeared briefly then headed back to safety.

Steve was concerned about the inadequacy of his cover. The hills were easy to climb and he was certain that in a matter of minutes riders would manage the climb on both sides of the break, leaving him and Amos at their mercy.

Dropping from his perch, Steve climbed back in the saddle, shouting to Amos to get behind again. With Amos hanging on, he sent Apache running for the top of the grade. He passed a deep fold that ran along the side of the hill each side of the break, and his heart skipped a beat as he saw a long line of Indians stretched out looking downhill over the brim. There was nothing for it but to keep going. The animal made level ground, and there, in front of him was a group of Indians on horseback, motionless, and another fifty or so horses, obviously belonging to the men who lay in wait behind him.

The Indians made no hostile moves, and the chief, a deep-chested, fine-featured Comanche placed his finger over his lips to indicate silence. Steve pulled Apache to a stop and made the gestures of greeting the Sequoia had shown him. The chief returned the greeting, then gestured for Steve and Amos to follow him. Dismounting, the chief led the two men to the brim of the hill, where he lay at full length to watch the men riding up the hillside each side of the break.

Steve made out five riders, three of them

immediately below and two on the other side of the break. They were intent upon outflanking the position he had held when gunning one of their number down. The man who had turned back was pointing to the approximate place. They were McCord's men all right, and Steve had no compassion for them as he sensed the Indians taking aim, some with rifles, some with bows and arrows. He recognised Caleb Hook at the moment the man's nostrils warned him what his instincts had told him moments earlier. Hook had always been able to smell out Indians, and a second before the hail of arrows and bullets scythed their way downhill, he had hauled his mount around in a swerving run towards the plain.

Amos was firing with as much enthusiasm as the Indians when Steve turned to the chief, gesturing and jabbering in halting Comanche to indicate the man who rode Indian fashion away from the scene, and that he wanted him for himself. The other four men succumbed to the fusillade, and the chief nodded his assent, sending Steve running for his mount.

Hurling himself astride Apache, he drove for the break. He had a flashing glimpse of raised spears saluting him on his way, and he thanked the Providence that had led him to find the wounded Sequoia down on the Neuces.

Caleb Hook was relieved to find the Indians had not taken up pursuit, and the fact that he was pursued by Steve Grant worried him not at all. In a one-to-one situation Hook felt he had the edge. Just a quarter of a mile away was the place to put his belief to the test. He remembered a fold in the ground that ran across the plain lowering the level by almost eight feet in a few yards. Spurring his mount heavily he upped the speed to get there ahead of his pursuer. When his mount checked to take the spine-jolting descent to the lower level, Caleb Hook slid out of the saddle and rolled away, gun in hand. His horse ran on.

When horse and rider had disappeared so rapidly from view, Steve remembered having wondered what had happened to the underlying strata for such a long uniform drop to have taken place, and his reaction was purely reflex.

Just before he reached the edge of the higher ground he dropped out of the saddle, allowing the lead rein to fall, bringing Apache to a stop. Then he was crawling, guns in hand, wide of where he had last seen Hook.

Caleb Hook smothered a curse as he realised his ruse had failed, then he crawled away to his left, his eyes glued to the top of the fold. He was too slow to counter the flying figure that hurtled over the top and landed feet first on his back. The breath left

Hook as Steve crashed into him, and he arched convulsively as Steve kept his feet and kicked out at the winded man's guns, sending them flying. Then Steve stood off, his guns levelled at the gasping, heaving man.

Steve waited a long time, while Caleb Hook fought for breath and cudgelled his brain for some way out of this totally unexpected impasse.

'Hook's the name, isn't it?' Steve said at length. 'Anyway that's what I heard McCord call you. Hook of Sheridan's Light Horse, eh? Killer of defenceless children, old men and women.'

Caleb Hook was staring at Steve out of pain-wracked eyes. 'You're talking about the war, feller. Sheridan's Light Horse was a fighting unit.'

'Yeah. Some of 'em did get to fighting, just to get the numbers depleted for the share-out. Well, I'm set on depleting the whole stinking lot of you. You'll make number fifteen, and if I keep up the scoring rate, then none of you scum will reach Nebraska.'

Caleb Hook was regaining his poise. Tough as a timber-wolf, he recovered quickly. 'So you're going to gun me down just like an executioner. That's murder in anybody's book.'

'Nope. You'll get your chance, Hook. Just stand up, and unbuckle your belt, let it drop and back away about twenty paces.'

Slowly, Hook complied. Steve replaced

one gun into its holster, and keeping the other level with Hook's breast, reached down for the belt, and finding Hook's guns, placed them in their holsters, then he threw the belt just in front of the now grinning man. 'Fasten it on, Hook, and go for your irons as fast as you like.' As he spoke, Steve slid his other gun into its holster and waited, alert, watchful.

'I'll tell McCord what you said when I get back, Grant,' Hook said sarcastically. 'When I tell him I saved his life killing you, he'll give me extra shares in the herd we'll steal outside Topeka and vote me another share of that loot we're supposed to have in Nebraska.'

Hook took his time fastening his belt, then slowly he fastened the thong of the left holster around his leg. He made to fasten the right holster, hoping to take Steve's attention, then quick as light, he hauled his favoured left-hand gun clear of the holster. Two shots rang out, the first bullet sent Hook's gun spinning, the second thudded into the man's evil heart.

Without a second glance at the dead man, Steve climbed the ridge, got into the saddle and collected Hook's horse. He hauled the corpse over the saddle and tied the man's body down, then fastening the lead rein to his own cantle, he rode off to the south-east. When he reckoned he had reached a point

that would be in the line of march for Mc-
Cord's wagon-train, he slipped the lead rein
and turned Apache back the way they had
come.

FIVE

'Well, I guess this'll do for the night,'
McCord said aloud. Mordant glanced at the
tiny tributary just ahead of them, that flowed
due east until it joined the Canadian River,
and grunted agreement. They dismounted
and waited for Zeke Rance to arrive with the
chuck-wagon. McCord peered to the north,
squinting as he quartered the horizon.
Mordant watched his chief, a sneer forming
on his face.

'Huh, a bit soon to expect Hook yet, I suppose,' McCord stated. 'A couple of hours
after dark should see him back.'

The chuck-wagon rolled up, followed by
the other wagons, forming a tight circle, and
shortly afterwards the remuda was picketed
downwind of the chuck-wagon.

Some time later they ate the meal Zeke
Rance had prepared, and while McCord
and Mordant stayed sitting on upturned
boxes near to the chuck-wagon, the others,
with the exception of the sentries who

62

circled the wagons, sat around the fire. The canvas of the long, low wagon was rolled back, and at each corner, a Gatling-gun was set up. Never again would McCord's camp get caught off-guard.

The men around the fire joked and laughed the first hour away, but as time passed they grew quiet. There was not one who cared a jot for Caleb Hook nor the other men who had set out after Steve Grant, but if Hook and his men failed to return, they would have lost fifteen of their number. At this rate, the odds on anyone around the fire reaching Topeka were mighty thin, leave alone Nebraska.

They smoked in silence for almost another hour and at last Eb Faulkner said what was in their minds.

'I reckon Caleb and the others have had their come-uppance. They'd have been back long ago if things had gone right.'

'Yeah. I guess you're right, Eb,' Lobo Dean replied. 'Six of 'em after two men, there's no sense to it. I always reckoned Hook was as good as any two men on his own.'

'Looks like it don't pay to separate from the main body any longer,' Jem Hammond put in. 'If the Major wants any hunting done from now on, he can do it himself for my part, and if any crowd goes into town from now, I'm going with 'em.'

The others digested Hammond's remarks

for a few minutes, then one after another, they voiced agreement. They all had a healthy regard for McCord's cold, cruel nature, but it now seemed that collectively bucking his word was safer than chasing the lethal shadows that dogged them.

McCord and Mordant kept their thoughts private. Mordant, particularly, was happy to envisage Hook dead. The seemingly indestructible Sergeant had always loomed doubtfully over Mordant's horizon, an obstacle to his total possession of the wealth awaiting him at the end of the trail.

McCord's iron self-discipline allowed him to settle down and sleep without further concern for Sergeant Hook and the others. He had the wagons rolling at daybreak, and an hour and a half later, he and Mordant saw the horse grazing desultorily with the burden draped over its saddle that they soon recognised as Caleb Hook. A few minutes later, upon examination, they took note of the hole plumb in the centre of Hook's heart, and the mutilated hand that had released the gun he had drawn.

'I guess we've got to face things,' Mordant said slowly. 'Grant is set on wiping out our every last man. I reckon he's got a large band of followers, and he's fooled us by seeming to be on his lonesome, or with just one other man, the black man that Hook mentioned. He must have drawn Hook into his trap.'

McCord shook his head decisively. 'I'm not saying that Grant hasn't got others helping him, but one thing's for sure, Hook died in a one-for-one fight.'

'More fool him for giving Grant an equal chance,' Mordant sneered at last, then as his agile mind considered his own skin, 'I think Grant requires your own special attention. With half of the men we've got left at your back, you'd outfox him in next to no time.'

Mordant's intentions were so transparent that McCord did not think the statement worth a reply. 'There'll be no more looking for Grant or anyone else,' he said. 'If we're going to grab a herd somewhere around Wichita, nobody's going farther away from camp than I can spit from here on.'

Long before Steve reached the break in the hills where he and Amos had run for safety he had given up wondering why the Comanches had taken sides in white man's troubles. He was a long way from the Neuces, Sequoia's hunting ground, and he found it hard to believe that the protection the young chief had promised would reach this far. As his mustang took the grade he scrutinized the hill each side of the break and he felt uneasy.

Reassurance flooded back as sentries and watchers showed here and there. He gained the top of the hill and saw, about four hundred yards away, the fires and tepees of the Indian camp. Riding in slowly, he saw a large circle of braves sitting around a fire in front of the tallest tepee. Dismounting, he picked out the tall, good-looking Indian chief sitting next to Amos, who seemed to be in good spirits.

The chief stood up and motioned Steve to join them. Steve and the chief stood face to face, then the chief clasped him in the manner of a blood-brother. 'You did what you had to do?' he questioned slowly in Comanche, and the Texan told him by halting speech and gestures what had happened. Not that the chief needed to be told. Scouts along the range of hills had watched, and Hook had barely bit the dust before the chief had been informed.

'It is good,' the chief replied. 'You are welcome to our camp, Steve Grant. I am Lone Bear. Let us eat, then we have a tepee for you both.'

'How did you know I am Steve Grant?' Steve asked, and a smile showed briefly on the chief's normally impassive features. He pointed to the eagle feathers in Steve's hatband.

'The notches show them to be the feathers given by Sequoia, son of Bald Eagle. Sequoia had to get the agreement of the Seven Family Chiefs of the Comanches to reward Steve Grant for the care and kindness shewn him. I am one of the Family

Chiefs. While you wear those feathers you have nothing to fear from any Comanche, Kiowa, Cheyenne, Ute, Crow or Sioux, you and those who travel with you.'

'You have given me the freedom of the plains, and you could well have saved our lives this night,' Steve replied. 'I will always be grateful.' The chief nodded his appreciation of Steve's slow, halting, but considered statement, then Steve continued. 'If you meet Sequoia, wish him well from me.'

Lone Bear nodded again and motioned Steve to be seated, then when they were sat cross-legged, he turned to the Texan. 'On the second day of the new moon, Sequoia and his family will assemble with us for the Sun Dance. Perhaps he will seek you out.'

Steve and Amos were drawn into the circle. Lone Bear's hospitality mirrored in the friendly attitude of the braves, who joked and indulged in horseplay; presenting an aspect of the Indian character that Steve found almost more than he could believe. When he settled down with Amos in their tepee for the night, he lay awake a long time puzzling over this universal misconception of the Indian character. Before he fell off to sleep, he decided that he would never take up arms against the Redman, and come what may, would always speak out in his defence.

Just after daybreak, Steve emerged from his tepee to find Lone Bear already sitting facing the fire. The braves were busy breaking camp. In the distance, near the rim of the hill, sentinels watched the plains below. Amos seemed to have found his own means of communication, and he was with seven or eight braves, all grinning and gesticulating as he tried his hand at packing away a tepee Comanche fashion. He finished to the apparent satisfaction of his tutors who laughingly indicated the tepees still standing and moved away as though leaving them to him, then thumped him playfully when they returned.

Lone Bear watched them, a benign expression on his face, then seeing Steve, indicated a place beside him. The chief told him to help himself to steaks that appeared to be burnt black and wheat cakes. The steak was delicious although the wheat cakes were dry to his taste.

After they had eaten, Lone Bear turned to Steve, his expression serious. 'It is time for us to go.' He stood up and a gesture from him had braves scurrying away to perform accustomed duties. His tepee was dismantled like magic, and another brave led Steve's horse and a sturdy, grey mustang that had seen Army service, to where Steve and Lone Bear stood. Amos made his farewells to the braves and joined Steve in thanking Lone Bear for his hospitality, and for coming to their help.

Without further ado Steve mounted Apache and Amos clambered astride the grey, then with a wave they set off to the north.

An hour's riding brought McCord's tail-end wagon into view and Steve decided to take a north-easterly course away from the line of wagons and direct to Oklahoma City for the Canadian River. As he changed direction Amos looked across, a question in his eyes.

'I've got a hunch that they'll all stick close to the wagons until they get over the shock of losing so many men. By the time they get to Oklahoma they'll have forgotten their losses and be ready for the saloons. We might as well ride ahead and get a night or two of rest before they arrive.'

'You know, Mister Steve,' Amos remarked, a slow smile on his face, 'You work things out like I was doing the thinking for you.'

'Glad you say so, Amos,' Steve rejoined with a grin.

They rode on companionably, content with the moment, and a couple of days later they rode into Oklahoma City.

With Caleb Hook buried, McCord ordered the wagon-train to get rolling again, and for another hour or more he and Mordant rode ahead, searching for the corpses of the other five men who had followed Hook. Finally they gave up looking. Whoever had killed them had either buried them or carted the bodies away.

It was a short step from that thought to the possibility that there were in fact no corpses. Maybe Hook had made up the story that Steve Grant was dogging them, intending to set off with his cronies for Nebraska. McCord and Mordant considered the men he had taken. Both Des Sayer and Sam Held had made the journey to Nebraska, and whereas Hook might have believed he had the loyalty of these men, they more likely had decided to dispense with Hook so that they could suit themselves.

McCord's thoughts went further back to the night in Matson, when the men at the camp had been killed, and he mulled over things before casting a quizzical glance at his lieutenant. 'You remember the night in Matson, Mordant?' he asked in his clipped tones. 'We were spread about a bit. There were no more than five of our men in the "Pony Express" with us all night. We sent Stuckey out to round them up about ten minutes before we left for camp.'

'Yeah, that's so,' agreed Mordant.

'So, there was nothing stopping some of our men hightailing back to camp and doing the killing. It would have presented no problems, because it wouldn't have been expected. And that would explain how seven

70

men died without themselves claiming a victim.'

The light in Mordant's eyes told McCord his lieutenant's thinking ran parallel to his own, as he continued. 'It's my belief Caleb Hook planned that, to get us jittery, and was aiming to use Grant as the red-herring to leave our ranks and beat us to Nebraska. He slipped up because Sayer and Held knew the route equally well. So in my book, we've got five men on the loose, hell-bent for Nebraska.'

'It makes sense,' Mordant said quietly. 'Those blamed fools could sure spoil everything. I reckon I should take a few men and ride 'em down.'

McCord's hard expression and curt shake of the head dismissed that suggestion. Hardly another word passed between them again until McCord settled upon a camping site for the night.

'I'd say we've got about two hundred and twenty miles ahead of us to Wichita, where we could get ourselves a herd. Sagar and Held will be expecting us to take about eight or nine days to Wichita so they won't push too hard.' McCord glanced at Mordant who nodded agreement. 'We could sell a herd at Topeka and still get to Nebraska first. By changing horses at shorter intervals we can make Wichita in four days. It's up to you, Mordant, to keep them rolling.'

'We'll make it in four days, that's for sure,' Mordant replied. 'I'll tell 'em what they can expect from sun-up tomorrow.'

Steve and Amos spent two days in Oklahoma City waiting for McCord and his men to show up, but they concluded the wagon-train had given Oklahoma City a wide berth, so they pressed on, and two days later rode into the little township of Enid.

They slowed their mounts to walking pace, taking in all that Enid had to offer. It wasn't much, unless one had an insatiable thirst, a liking for poker or faro, a penchant for the ladies or a gut desire to fight some drunken slob at every turn. Just a long, frame-fronted Main Street, bisected by a shorter road with tumble-down houses, smithy and Court-house. The livery-stable was at the north end of town, where they headed, and over all lay a thick pall of dust. Punchers and drovers lined the sidewalks, irresolute, as though debating whether to push their way back into the bulging saloons, or get to heck out of it.

The drovers had money to burn. Most of them had been paid at Topeka after long, hard drives, and after the first celebrations at Topeka, they had kept their plans to take full pokes home for many miles, but Enid was just the right distance from Topeka to spoil the best of intentions.

The pardners rode the length of Main Street to the livery-stable, where a harassed oldster told them to see to their own broncs. When asked the likeliest place to find a room, he said with some asperity, 'The broncs had the best rooms in this hyar burg.'

Leaving the livery-stable, the two men made their way back along the length of Main Street, looking for a hotel. There were three hotels of dubious quality, filled with humanity, and considering the numbers of men lining the sidewalks, Steve reckoned that the saloons would be filled day and night, so the prospects of getting a bed in Enid looked decidedly slim.

Amos found nothing in his new surroundings to cheer him. 'This place Enid, Mister Steve, is the most evil-looking place I've ever seen.' He shot a hopeful look at Steve. 'So the sooner you decide to move on, the better I'll like it.'

'Yeah. I guess you're right, Amos, we'll just take a looksee into the saloons, and if there's no hide nor hair of McCord's outfit we'll hit the trail.'

Mollified, Amos' face broke into its customary grin, and together they embarked on the search of every saloon. It was a long, hot, unpleasant task. Pushing through the throng of sweating revellers, turning aside the attentions of predatory women, apologising for bumping into some hot-eyed men still

73

sober enough to have itchy fingers, and refusing steadfastly to assuage their own thirsts with long, cool drinks that Enid provided from an apparently endless supply. They came out of the last saloon, beside the staging-depot, when the Stage rolled in from Arkansas.

'Here ma'am, take a drink of this. It'll put some colour back in your cheeks.' The rotund drummer held out his flask toward the girl who was seated in the opposite corner of the swaying Stage. She made an effort to smile her thanks but did not quite manage to make it. She shook her head, and Sam Hodder accepted the rebuff philosophically. He was about to take a pull himself when the brash-looking young gambler sitting next to the girl, reached for the flask, taking it from Hodder's podgy grasp.

'I guess it'll do me more good than the lady. I don't think you sell enough in a year to thaw this little gal. Maybe tonight in Enid they won't wait for her to thaw any. They don't reckon to take no for an answer.' Mart Roper turned his sardonic grin at Jill Rankin and leered wolfishly. 'Like I've told you, you'd better let me look out for you the two days you've got to wait in Enid.'

Anger flooded Jill Rankin's lovely features as she glared at Roper. 'I doubt that I'll find anyone in Enid so lacking in gentlemanly conduct as you.' She looked around the other occupants of the coach but there was no help to be found amongst them. Sam Hodder was kindly enough to want to help, but he knew his limitations. The other three travellers had never helped anyone but themselves, and anyway, they were catching up on sleep because they didn't reckon on much for the next two nights in Enid.

Roper edged a bit closer to the girl, his face hard. 'I guess you're right lady, I'm no gentleman, but there's one thing for sure, you ain't going to find a gentleman any-where in Enid, and no bed neither. The only way you'll get a bed in Enid is sharing it with a man.' Jill's face and neck were brick-red by this time, but he went on, 'More than likely you'll get a steady procession of men throughout the night. Take my offer and at least you'll do the best for yourself.'

Fire suddenly snapped from the girl's eyes as she mastered her feelings and turned to look the young gambler squarely in the face. 'Any woman could do without your sort of help, Mister. Anyway. You bother me any more and I'll put a bullet where your brain ought to be.'

Roper's expression slipped a little and his face visibly paled as he realized her left hand held a wicked-looking Derringer. 'You've sure enough got gall, lady,' Roper drawled. He searched her face with eyes like ice chips, but she matched him glare for glare. 'Maybe – yeah, just maybe, you'd use that thing.'

'Oh, there's no maybe. You step out of line one more time and you're dead.'

'We're four hours out of Enid, lady. You're going to be mighty tired keeping that toy pointing at me.'

'There's no move you can make from here on, Mister, that'll outspeed the first bullet out of the toy – which incidentally, does a lot more damage than a .45.'

Roper eased away, and as the minutes slid by, tried to regain his composure. 'God-dammit,' he thought. 'How in Hades did I judge this dame wrong, she's got more iron than most hombres.' He transferred his attentions to the nearby hills but he became more and more aware of the nearness of this good-looking girl with the mean streak. He'd get his chance when she arrived in Enid to find it was all that he had said.

SIX

Jack Bennett dropped down from the driving seat of the Stage, bashed his hat a few times on his knee to clear the dust from it, and opened the Stage-door before clambering back up to the roof-rack via the driving-seat.

76

A couple of middle-aged men clambered out followed by Sam Hodder, the drummer, then another middle-aged man before Mart Roper leapt to the ground. The last occupant put her head out of the coach and looked around at the sidewalks of Enid as Steve and Amos drew level. There was apprehension in her glance which caught Steve's attention, and as she held on to the door-frames to make a footing on the first step, he was struck by the overall picture of prettiness she made. Her face was lightly tanned, oval, with big, dark blue eyes, small nose and shapely, generous mouth. The hair that peaked beneath a wide hat was titian red. She was dressed in a two-piece in black, with collar to the neck; hip length, shaped top piece, with skirt almost to the ground. She got to the road and moved aside as the other passengers grabbed their cases from Bennett, who held them one after another overside.

The loungers on the sidewalks came to life, and crowded the rail to stare unashamedly at the good-looking girl. One after another they shouted their invitations to her, some of the things being said making Steve burn with anger. For one fleeting moment he caught her glance and he saw the distress in her eyes. Then Roper took a hand.

He reached for his case, and slung it on the sidewalk, then, seeing the girl had returned the Derringer to wherever she kept it, he grabbed her around the waist with her arms pinioned, picked her off the ground and whirled her around a couple of times, then planted a kiss full on her lips. He kept her aloft and shouted to the men on the sidewalk.

'You fellers hold your horses. This gal is mine, and anyone forgetting the fact gets to Boot Hill.'

Roper had been to Enid often enough to have forged a reputation, and the crowd pretty soon found interest elsewhere. The girl was pretty right enough, but dying for a woman when a man was rebuilding a thirst was plain crazy.

As Roper placed Jill's feet back on the ground, he stared stonily at her as he spoke. 'So now you know what I told you is true. There's no other women in Enid except the sort that sell themselves, and you can't hold off that lot,' he nodded towards the sidewalk. 'Now grab your case and come with me. I've got a bed and you can share it.'

Steve hadn't heard what Roper said to the girl as the man released her. He saw her eyes flood with tears of rage and frustration, then as she looked towards the sidewalk unadulterated fear took over. Steve vaulted over the rails and landed between Jill and the rangy-looking Roper. He gave Roper a bland look before turning to the girl.

'Seems to me you're in some sort of trouble, ma'am,' Steve said slowly. 'Have you got folks here to visit or are you just riding through?'

Jill looked at Steve squarely and hope flooded back into her. 'No, Mister. I'm riding on, but the next Stage south is in two days.'

'Well – you've heard how it is, feller,' Roper snarled. 'So hit the skyline.'

'So you've got no place to stay?' Steve persisted, ignoring Roper.

The driver was about to get in front to drive the Stage away. Steve held on to his arm, and Jack Bennett turned and waited for Steve to speak.

'You the owner of this Line?' and when Bennett nodded, 'Then you've got a place here where a girl can stay in safety?'

Bennett looked at the girl for the first time with any degree of interest. Most women coming into Enid were nothing but trouble, but he could see this one was different. 'Yeah, I've got a couple of rooms, and my wife would be happy for a chat, likewise you can have the other room if you want.'

'That'll do fine.' Steve smiled his agreement. 'I'll have to double up in my room, I've got a friend on the sidewalk.' He nodded to Amos. Both the girl and the driver took in Amos, but they didn't seem to notice his colour.

'Thank you both!' Jill said, relief flooding through her. 'Oh, thank you!'

Roper's face was a study. He was being

outsmarted. The men on the sidewalk were taking interest again, and suddenly Roper felt his reputation was at stake. He stepped forward, placing his hand on Steve's shoulder, swinging him around. 'I told you to hightail it, Mister!' he snarled. 'If you've got any other ideas, then you'd better be able to back them up.'

'I've got my own ideas sure,' Steve said quietly, 'So why don't you crawl away to the gopher hole you came from?'

Men moved away out of the line of fire as the two men stood close, each weighing up the other. Steve knew Roper's type, and guessed the man had killed many times when he could as easily have turned away from trouble, whereas Roper could not believe the man standing four-square in front of him was any real threat to his reputation as a gunman. He made his mind up quickly and went for his guns. They were still in his holsters when Steve's right fist exploded in his face, sending him crashing to the ground, to lie inert, out to the world.

Steve crossed over to the unconscious man with the appreciative shouts of the crowd in his ears, and, taking out the man's guns, he emptied both chambers before tossing them back beside him.

'You pack a mean punch, Mister,' Jack Bennett said, as he surveyed Roper thoughtfully. 'Well, get yourselves aboard and I'll take you around to my place.'

Steve ushered Jill and Amos aboard, and hauled the girl's suitcase into Amos' keeping before taking his place inside. Bennett got going, driving off Main Street at the intersection, then around the back of the Stage-line office to the courtyard and stabling, and the house that stood beyond the stables.

Bennett climbed down as Steve opened the door of the Stage and dropped to the ground. He waited while the younger man hauled the girl down, and Amos followed the girl, carrying her suitcase. 'C'mon, I'll take you inside before I see to the broncs.'

Sarah Bennett was a plump, motherly soul of about forty-five who took the influx of guests without batting an eyelid, and as her husband briefly outlined the circumstances she nodded and placed a consoling arm around Jill's shoulders. 'Come on, my dear, I'll show you to your room so that you can freshen up some before eating.'

Jill murmured her thanks, and catching Steve's eye smiled her thanks to him. He returned it with a friendly grin that chased away every vestige of severity, and made his strong features almost handsome. As she climbed the stairs she fought down the impulse to take another look at him, but she couldn't cast aside the picture imprinted on her mind. She decided she definitely liked the look of the stranger who had smoothed

81

away her troubles.

Sarah Bennett came back down and stood for a moment with arms folded, taking in both Amos and Steve. 'I'm Sarah Bennett,' she said. 'What do I call you?'

'I'm Amos, ma'am.'

'And I'm Steve Grant.'

Sarah nodded, and with the introductions done she pointed the way to a door leading out of the big living-room. 'The bedroom's in there, so you can share. And if you want to freshen up you'll find the pump outside.'

'We're much obliged to you, ma'am,' Steve said. 'Seems there are too many folk crowding Enid for comfort.'

A cloud appeared in the woman's eyes as she replied. 'Yes, far too many, and all the wrong sort. Most of the folk who settled when we did have moved on. Since the railhead for cattle opened at Topeka everything's changed. It seems that every herder stops off at Enid to spend his profits or wages, and every footloose card-sharp, gunman or dancer flood in to take their money away. If my husband wasn't so stubborn we'd move on as well.' She pulled herself together and gave them a quick smile. 'That's enough of my troubles, get yourselves settled in and I'll have a meal ready for you pretty soon.'

The two men nodded and made their way into the next room, which they discovered to be quite sizeable, with two beds, washstand, slim wardrobes and a square of Navajo rug in the centre of the floor.

When Steve and Amos returned to the living-room, sluiced and generally tidied up, Jack Bennett was there talking to the girl. Bennett motioned them to seats, but before they could sit Jill Rankin came forward impulsively. She lifted her beautiful dark-blue eyes to look Steve straight in the face, her face serious.

'I'd like to thank you for getting me out of trouble, Mister-er–' She tailed off as that captivating smile spread across his face.

'Grant, ma'am – Steve Grant. But you've no call to be beholden. It just happened we were there, if it hadn't been us, it would have been someone else.'

'No, Mister Grant,' Jill broke in. 'I don't think anyone else would have taken sides against that gunman on my account.' She paused, as she realized she should complete the formalities. 'My name is Jill Rankin.'

'Pleased to meet you, Miss Rankin,' Steve held his hand out as he spoke, engulfing her slim hand in his broad palm. He nodded towards Amos. 'And this is my pard, Amos.'

When Steve released her hand she shook Amos' hand in turn. 'Glad to know you, Miss Rankin,' Amos said, 'And I'm mighty pleased that Mister Steve was on hand when you needed help.'

The girl's name stuck in Steve's mind, and

his scrutiny when she took a seat brought a warm flush rising from her neck to her cheeks. 'Rankin,' Steve said aloud. Her straight look as he uttered her name again held a quality that he remembered. 'Are you on your way to Waco from Wichita?'

Jill's eyes opened in amazement. 'Yes I am! How did you know?'

'Your father, Dave Rankin, runs the store in Waco, isn't that so?'

'Why, yes,' she replied. 'You know him?'

Steve nodded. 'I knew he intended sending for you. Why didn't you wait?'

'I got fed up with waiting. Five years is a long time. But you must know my father pretty well for him to have told you he'd be sending for me.'

'Yeah. It's my store, Miss Rankin.'

'Well, what do you know!' Jack Bennett ejaculated. 'Kinda funny you people meeting the way you did, when you were all set to meet in Waco anyway.'

'Sure was providential,' Amos said.

'Who takes the Stage on from here, Mister Bennett?' Steve transferred his attention to the driver.

'Call me Jack,' Bennett said quickly, then, 'Sam Munro's got the franchise from Enid to Oklahoma, then Wells Fargo carries on south.'

'It's pretty rough country between here and Oklahoma,' Steve mused. 'Too rough for a girl to travel on her own.' He looked directly at Jill, and his face was stern. 'So you're going to take the next Stage back to Wichita.'

'Can't see that'll help the young lady,' Bennett broke in. 'From here to Wichita's no better than from here to Oklahoma.'

'We'll be riding right alongside, all the way to Wichita,' Steve said with finality. 'And when we've finished our business, we'll ride from Wichita to Waco with the Stage.'

Bennett glanced at the girl, and what he saw was mutinous disagreement.

'I'll thank you not to make plans for me, Mister Grant,' Jill said decisively. 'I really can take care of myself. That man travelled the last four hours to Enid with my gun keeping him quiet, and I would have killed him myself, given time.'

Steve took a closer look at the girl. Beautiful she certainly was, but there was no denying the steadiness in her eyes. He admitted to himself that she was sufficiently strong-willed to kill rather than submit.

'Miss Rankin,' he said, 'I don't doubt your ability to look after yourself in ordinary circumstances, but don't forget, now that we've met, your father would hold me responsible for you, and I don't intend to take that responsibility lightly. I don't care what you say, I'm taking you back to Wichita until I'm ready to take you all the way to Waco. What do you think, Amos?'

'I think that Miss Rankin would be well advised to do what you say for her father's sake.'

Sarah Bennett bustled in from the kitchen at that moment. She gave a quick look at the three newcomers. 'I hope you've all got good appetites. I'll have it ready in a couple of minutes if you'll take your seats.'

They murmured assent to having good appetites and Steve moved straight away to the table, and held out a chair for the girl to sit. Steve motioned Amos to one side of her and took the seat on the other side.

Sarah was a first-rate cook and managed to produce in all of them a satisfied torpor, so when next Steve broached the time of the next coach out north for Wichita, Jill made no demur. Told that the coach would leave the day after tomorrow, Steve and Amos seemed satisfied, and Jill gave no indication of her feelings.

Lying awake in a comfortable bed, Jill relived the events of the day, and she found that Steve Grant's face and sturdy frame took precedence over the others who had conspired to make the day memorable. Despite his dictatorial manner, she could not help but feel gratified for his concern, and his acceptance of responsibility to her father. Just before falling asleep, she also admitted to herself that she liked him.

Mart Roper was outside the Stage-line office at sun-up, settling himself for relaxed action when the Oklahoma Stage arrived from the stables. He was expecting Jill Rankin to join the Stage and maybe the man who had come to her rescue would be on hand to see her off. Roper's ego was dented, and the only way to wipe the slate clean was to send the man to Boot Hill with his usual expertise. One thing was sure, there would be no chance of the man escaping by throwing a lucky punch.

The Stage-line office opened, Lee Bowen the clerk making three attempts to find the keyhole. It always took a sizeable jolt from the office bottle of bourbon to get his vision straight after his once-a-week bender. He walked through into the partitioned office, and measured out his drink before throwing the customer window open. Checking the list, he noted just three passengers, the mail and a dozen items of freight, then took his seat behind the window.

Ten minutes later Sam Munro brought the Oklahoma Stage to a stop outside the office and tied the lead-horse to the hitchrail. While he waited for the passengers he made three journeys to and from the Stage with the freight.

In due course, three men entered the office to check in, and Mart Roper's eyes were everywhere. The girl should be here any second, and with any luck the hombre who had his come-uppance due.

With the departure time for the Stage approaching, the sidewalks were filling up, so Roper stepped off the sidewalk and stood beside the Stage, keeping the whole town under surveillance.

At last the three men took their places in the Stage, and a couple of minutes later Sam Munro unhitched the lead-horse, and climbing up, picked up the reins and with a shout sent his team on the south run, spewing dust in a thick cloud.

Roper felt his anger rising like a flood, and running up the steps to the sidewalk, pushed into the Stage-line office. Lee Bowen looked at him through the pigeon-hole owlishly. 'Where in heck did your other passenger get to?' Roper asked.

'What other passenger?' Bowen asked in turn, then when Roper did not immediately answer, 'There were only three passengers booked.'

Roper stared in disbelief. 'Where's that woman who came in two days ago from Arkansas? She was due to carry on to Waco.'

Bowen smiled. He had no liking for Roper, so he took pleasure in bringing the man up to date. 'Oh, Miss Rankin, you mean. She left yesterday morning for Wichita, and Grant, the hombre who slugged you, and that black pardner of his rode out with the Stage. Jack

Bennett told me they'll be riding alongside the lady clear through to Wichita.'

Roper stood stock-still, glaring at Bowen. 'Let's see the passenger list for yesterday's Arkansas run!' he barked. 'Bowen shrugged and reached for the clipboard of passenger lists. He thrust it through the pigeon-hole and Roper snatched it up. A couple of minutes later Roper made up his mind. He tossed the clipboard through to Bowen's desk then hurried out to the sidewalk, made some purchases at the store, and after collecting his saddle-bags headed for the livery to purchase a horse and take the northern trail.

SEVEN

'Must be four thousand head in that herd,' McCord remarked. 'Prime stock too. They've been trail-herded right. They'll fetch a good price at Topeka.'

Mordant looked across the quarter-mile gap to the front markers of the herd. 'Yeah, all of our thousand,' he replied. 'That herd would suit us fine. Pity we're not closer to Topeka.'

'They could stand losing a bit of meat,' McCord observed. 'But not what they'd shed at the speed we'd have to hustle 'em.

No, we'll have to chance what we can pick up just a couple of days out of Topeka.'

'Well, we're making good time,' Mordant said. 'We'll have no trouble picking up a herd for sale in Topeka and deal with Held and Sagar this side of Nebraska.'

They rode in silence for a few minutes, then Mordant posed the question that had crossed his mind time and time again. 'If things go the way we expect, how are we going to explain away the fact that nobody else returns off furlough?'

McCord shrugged his shoulders. 'It's not up to us to explain. General Sheridan knows we intended herding a drive to Topeka, so nobody at Headquarters will be surprised that rankers with money to burn could not be bothered to report back just to sign off.'

Mordant digested this and although he made no reply, he was satisfied that Mc-Cord was right.

Later, when the last of the light was fading, and Zeke Rance had the meal about ready, Eb Faulkner rode in from drag with another rider in tow. They dismounted just outside the ring of wagons and Faulkner led the way between two wagons and approached Mc-Cord and Mordant who stood near to the fire. Their cold eyes appraised the newcomer as he came to a stop.

'Name's Roper,' Faulkner said laconically. 'Fancied some company for the night.

Mister McCord and Mister Mordant.'

Roper nodded and thrust out his hand. McCord took a long time to shake the proffered hand as he studied Roper, assessing him in his cold clinical way. Mordant just nodded coolly, and made no attempt to shake hands.

'Where're you heading?' McCord asked without preamble.

'North,' replied Roper unhelpfully, and he now had a hard look on his face.

McCord knew a gunslinger when he saw one, so he allowed a smile to stretch his lips. 'Well, you're welcome to share the fire and chow.' He motioned to the upturned boxes around the fire and he and Mordant sat down, leaving one between them for Roper.

The rest of the crew crowded around when Zeke Rance yelled the message that the meal was ready, and one after another they took their places around the fire with piled plates and mugs steaming with coffee.

'That sure was good,' Roper said at length, after he had drained the last dregs of coffee. 'You've got yourself a mighty good cook there.'

'Yeah, he can turn out a good meal at the drop of a hat,' McCord agreed. He offered a cheroot to Roper, who took it with an appreciative nod.

They smoked in comfortable silence until McCord reckoned Roper was mellowed some, then he posed the question again. 'Just where north are you heading, Roper?' The gambler decided the meal was worth an explanation.

'In the general direction of Wichita, I guess,' he said, then looking directly at Mc-Cord continued. 'I reckon you've been close to the Wichita trail in the last couple of days, so maybe you can tell me how far ahead the Stage is.'

McCord shook his head. 'No, we've seen no sign of it. What's so special about the Stage?'

'The Stage isn't so special,' Roper replied. 'There's a hombre accompanying that coach to Wichita. He crossed me in Enid and got lucky. I'm going to see his luck runs out somewhere on the trail or in Wichita. They had a day lead of me out of Enid.'

'This hombre's riding with the Stage, you say,' McCord mused. 'Must be something on the Stage mighty important to him to make him ride shotgun.'

Roper laughed a brittle laugh. 'Yeah. A woman. She had booked out of Wichita for Waco, but there was a two-day wait at Enid. Well, it seems this hombre, Grant, per-suaded her to go back to Wichita until he could travel with her to Waco. Him and his black pardner.'

A quick looked passed between McCord and Mordant. 'This Grant, he must come from Waco then?' McCord put in quickly.

Roper cast a sharp glance at McCord. 'It sounds like you know him,' he said.

'If his name is Grant, coming from Waco, riding a bay stallion and partnered by a blackman, then we know him,' McCord said firmly. 'If you're tracking him, Roper, you must be some artist with those six-guns of yours.'

'What's so special about him?' Roper asked.

'We saw him in action once in Waco, and he's fast and cool, very cool.'

Roper was silent a long time, mulling over the events up to the blow Grant had thrown that had forestalled a gun battle. As he remembered, Grant had been cool. Well, he had killed a lot of cool men in his time. He finished his cheroot and stood up. 'If it's all right by you I'll get some shuteye under one of your wagons, so I can make an early start. I intend to see just how good Grant is.'

As Roper passed beyond the firelight, significant looks passed between McCord and Mordant; then when the other men formed into their customary groups around the fire, the two men drew back into the shadows to discuss the new situation.

'So! Hook was right!' Mordant said. 'He said Grant was in tow with a black hombre.'

'Yeah, and if Grant was in Enid, then he must have killed Hook and the others. Now

93

Roper says he's taking a woman bound for Waco, his home town, back to Wichita until he's free to make the journey to Waco with her. That means he's got business either in Wichita or some place north of Wichita.' McCord paused, while he lit another cheroot. 'I've got a feeling we're his business.'

'How come?' Mordant asked. He believed McCord was right, but he wanted the reasoning behind the other's statement.

'He's got the stamp of military about him, and he's a Southerner, so he could be an agent following us to find out where we cached all the loot we took out of those houses down south.'

'And whittling us down on the way,' Mordant put in. 'Do you think he's acting for the Army or for the big southern estate owners?'

McCord shook his head, momentarily puzzled. 'I don't know. He might just have his own reasons, but whichever, he's done too darned well for my liking.'

'Maybe we ought to give Roper some help,' Mordant said.

McCord pulled out a map from the inside pocket of his jacket, then crossing to the fire-light he studied the map a long time before returning to the seat beside Mordant.

'I think you're right,' McCord said finally. 'We'd better give Roper a bit of help. He may be pretty sharp with those guns of his, but although he says Grant got lucky last time it's my belief that Roper got lucky. So I don't think Roper's going to solve any of our problems on his lonesome. I don't intend to split our numbers for the chore either, so we'll all get after the Stage.' He paused to light a cheroot, then continued, 'Roper said the Stage left a day before him, so it can't be far away now. Right now I reckon they're spending the night at Maken Creek, and that's no more than twenty miles away. Then they'll have fifty miles to Wichita with either a stop-over at Manitou or a change of horses. I reckon we can be close to Maken Creek by the time they head out for Manitou.'

'Might be as well to let Roper try his hand first when we get close enough to the Stage,' Mordant said quietly. 'No sense in us showing our hand if he's going to get lucky. If I remember right, the terrain alters a lot beyond Maken Creek, right through on up to Topeka, with canyons, arroyos, and close-set hills breaking up the plains. Whatever we do in that territory could well be seen by hombres under cover.'

McCord nodded. Mordant made sense, but then, he always did.

'Yeah, we'll do that,' McCord answered. 'Let 'em know what we intend.' He indicated the card players with a gesture. 'And I'll palaver with Roper. Let him know he's on to a thousand dollars for killing Grant and his sidekick, and we'll be on hand to pay on the nose. I guess four hours' sleep will do us for now.'

Mordant nodded his agreement and crossed to where the men were still playing cards, and in his usual brusque manner passed on McCord's intentions, ending by demanding they get some sleep immediately. Nobody demurred. They were eager enough to see Roper bring down the man who had dogged them so disastrously all the way from Waco.

McCord found Roper quite prepared to travel along with the wagon-train, and most receptive to the idea that McCord should pay him one thousand dollars for a chore he intended completing anyway.

Steve and Amos pulled up outside the Maken Creek Stage office, and, tying their mounts to the hitchrail, stomped into the office to give Jack Bennett a hand with the packages and mail. Bennett grinned to himself. He knew durned well that Steve was driven more by his desire to spend a bit of time with Jill Rankin than help the Stage on its way. The girl came into the waiting-room at that moment and nodded her greeting coolly.

Jill had acceded to Steve's demand to return to Wichita, but she was determined to show she was travelling under duress. She had maintained a prim disinclination to talk, and confined herself to monosyllabic replies to every attempt by Steve to thaw her out. When Amos spoke to her she replied eagerly, in like vein, and she behaved normally with the other three passengers.

Contrary to her apparent uninterest in Steve's existence, she found herself watching for him as he rode with Amos, sometimes ahead, sometimes wide out on the flanks, and sometimes alongside Jack Bennett, the driver. She liked the handsome set of his features in profile, the rugged dependability suggested in his powerfully set shoulders, and his lithe, easy movements. She was drawn to him irresistibly, so contrarily, she tried all the harder to prove he was of no consequence to her.

'Soon have you safe in Wichita now,' Steve remarked airily, as he prepared to make his way outside with some packages.

Jill had to cut the light from her eyes as she replied. 'Yes! And thanks to you I've got the journey all to do again. By this time I'd have been near half-way to Waco.'

Steve grinned disarmingly. 'Yeah, it must seem a bit hard on you. We'll have to make the journey back more interesting. Maybe you'd like to make the ride in the saddle, rather than in a stuffy coach?'

Despite herself the excitement showed in her eyes. 'Do you think I could?'

'Sure thing. We'll pick out the right cayuse for you.' The other passengers arrived as Steve replied, and there was a general movement out of the office. Jill made to leave, then turned impulsively to face Steve.

'Yes, Mister Grant. I'd like very much to ride to Waco on horseback, and I've got my own horse in Wichita. I never wanted to leave her anyway.'

When she took her place in the Stage, she looked for Steve as he mounted Apache, and as he rode around the coach to catch sight of her before joining Amos out in front, she gave him the first involuntary smile.

Jack Bennett was just about to shout his team on its way when a rider, in from the north, stopped alongside him. 'You want to keep a sharp lookout, driver,' he yelled. 'The hills are crawling with Indians.'

'Where did you see 'em?' asked Bennett.

'All the way from Wichita,' the puncher replied. 'It could be they're just making their way home after the Sun Dance, but I saw too many for comfort. Seems like Cheyenne, Crow, and Kiowa, but I didn't get close enough to be sure.'

'I'm sure obliged to you, feller,' Bennett said. 'I'll be looking out for 'em.' With an appreciative wave, the driver shook the reins and gave his customary shout to get the Stage under way.

When they cleared Maken Creek, Bennett

gave a shout to Steve and Amos who were just ahead, and when they allowed the Stage to catch up, he passed on what the puncher had said. Neither appeared to be disturbed at the news, so the Stage-line owner relaxed. When the pards moved on again they took far wider order, nearer the foothills that crowded in ever closer order to the trail.

Beyond the foothills, the mountain range that for so long had been just a backdrop to the undulating endless plain, took shape and character, peak after snow-capped peak, with dark faces of shadow showing where vertical walls stole the sunlight. Farther to the east the plains continued, seemingly endless, but west, beyond the Arkansas River, the country had taken on a new look, mean, bleak and forbidding.

As they were running through the first long canyon out of Maken Creek, Steve felt his sixth-sense working overtime. He knew as surely as he knew his own name that they were being watched. When they ran clear of the canyon he had the evidence of his own eyes to reinforce his sixth-sense. There was plenty of movement on the ridges of the hills that dominated the lefthand side of the trail. Amos, whose only brush with Indians evoked happy memories, watched the horsemen on the ridges with his customary benevolent expression. Steve caught the expression and the direction of the older man's gaze.

'They don't look too hostile, Amos,' he said. 'But there's plenty of them. Enough to hide some braves with a fancy for scalps given the chance. We'll just have to watch for any quick moves.'

'We found them friendly last time, Mister Steve, I can't see why they should be any different now.'

'Just remember, Amos,' Steve answered. 'Most whites are decent, law-abiding folk, but you've met plenty of bad ones. Well, there are renegades of every colour, so you can't trust your life to them all. I expect you've known plenty of bad blackmen in your time.'

Amos thought about it a bit then replied, 'Yes, I guess you're right, Mister Steve. There've been blackmen I wouldn't turn my back on.'

Three hours out of Maken Creek, Jack Bennett pulled into the little huddle of wooden huts that was Chocataw, for a change of horses, and some hard tack and coffee that was always available from old Lionel Slade, who bred some good quality broncs in Chocataw Valley. Indians had watched them every step of the way, but none of them had shown warlike intent.

Jack Bennett asked Slade about them as they ate their meal, and the old horse-breeder gave the general company the benefit of his beady glance. 'Oh, they've been on the move since yesterday morning,' he said. 'They've been celebrating the Sun Dance, and they're making their way back to their own villages. It's a good sign when they leave the celebrations peacefully.' He took a closer look at the crossed feathers Steve wore in the band of his sombrero, then continued. 'Still, you hombres should get no trouble this run anyway, not while Grant's riding along.'

'How come?' Jack Bennett asked.

'I've known one other man who wore the crossed eagle feathers as of right, and there wasn't a Plains Indian who wouldn't respect him and anyone he happened to be with.'

Old Slade's words had Bennett and his passengers eyeing Steve curiously, and Jill Rankin had to stifle the interest the old man's words had raised in her; but Steve merely shrugged the remark away, and took his hard tack and coffee into the open air. Amos started to follow him then thought better of it. He looked around the others, and sat back down.

'It's right like you say, Mister,' Amos said quietly. 'Just a few days ago we were in deep trouble, and I don't think we'd have gotten out of it, but Indians turned up out of nowhere and helped out. Made us welcome too until we moved on.' Having said his piece, he followed Steve outside, leaving the others pondering upon the reasons for

101

Steve's friendship with the Plain Indians.

When they were all ready to set off, Steve and Amos sat their mounts a hundred yards ahead of the Stage. Jill curbed her curiosity, deciding that Steve had purposely moved away so that he would not have to answer questions, and because of that she determined not to embarrass him when they were eventually thrown together.

It was about an hour and a half later that they saw a rider back-trail, travelling fast, apparently intent upon catching the Stage, and way behind, farther east, moving dust spoke of either a herd or wagons on the move. The Stage carried on its way, passengers and driver unaware of the pursuing rider. Steve and Amos waited, one each side of the trail, and hidden behind thick bushes of mesquite.

EIGHT

At sun-up McCord and his men had been on the move three hours and the little change-station of Chocataw was no more than eight miles away. McCord and Mordant rode alongside Roper, but Roper was in no mood for conversation. He rode, morose, smouldering inside at the fancied slight to his manhood at the hands of Steve Grant.

With the coming of the sun, McCord's interest in Roper faded. Five years had passed since his last treacherous slaughter of an Indian village, but time had not dimmed his ability to smell out Indians. The proof was there for all to see soon enough. Atop the ridges mounted Indians showed up, their horses positioned in varying postures, sending their own messages to their compatriots hidden from view.

Roper had eyes only for the sign the Stage had recently left behind. McCord drew the man's attention to the Indians. 'Those redskins are too close for comfort. We're going to leave you here, Roper, head the wagons farther east to give us room if they turn hostile. Maybe you'd better join us. You can still get even with Grant in Wichita.'

Roper gave a quick glance at the foothills, taking in the motionless riders spread along the ridges. 'Nope,' he said, 'You go and see to your wagons, maybe I'll join you when I'm done.'

McCord hauled his mount around without a word, Mordant followed close behind, as always.

As Roper rode through Chocataw, old Lionel Slade waved a greeting which Roper totally ignored. He felt excitement well up in him as the deep indentations in the dust told him that the Stage was very close. The wind had not yet started to fill in the ruts. He urged more speed out of his mount, staring ahead for the telltale dust cloud. When he saw the dust cloud, he was so intent upon it that he almost missed the two riders who emerged out of it briefly before taking cover each side of the trail behind the thorn bushes.

For a split second the grey rump of a horse showed at the back of the thicket on the right of the trail, and he remembered McCord's words. 'If his name is Grant, coming from Waco, riding a bay stallion, and partnered by a blackman, then we know him.' Grant was Roper's concern, and it seemed a million to one that Grant was waiting on the lefthand side of the trail. He palmed a gun into his right hand and primed himself for the first shot.

The thickets were now only a hundred yards away and Roper came on, seemingly intent upon catching the Stage. He was expecting the men in wait to ease onto the trail, but they did not. As he came abreast of the mesquite bushes Roper slid to the right of his mount, holding on Indian fashion. He had a brief glimpse of the rider on a bay horse turning to give chase, and he fired under the outstretched neck of his own mount.

The face of the rider showed as he started to slip from the saddle, and a surge of elation ran through Roper as he recognised Grant, and saw the blood on his face. He would have fired again, but he was left with no angle. As he guided his mount off the trail, he resumed his seat in the saddle, riding low over the animal's neck. A couple of shots rang out, but the bullets weren't close enough to worry about so he concentrated his attention on rejoining the wagon-train.

McCord watched Roper's racing return through his telescope, and he saw some Indians moving down towards the trail off the ridge. They weren't in sufficient numbers to cause concern.

Roper's face was flushed with success as he reined in his lathered mount. McCord and Mordant looked at him expectantly. 'Well!' he said at length. 'That was a whole lot easier than I reckoned on. Grant and that black hombre were hiding beside the trail waiting for me, but I saw 'em move into cover. They intended coming at me from behind, but I gunned down Grant just as he broke cover. Got him plumb in the forehead. That black pardner of his pumped a couple of shots in my direction but he was way off target.'

'What are your plans now?' McCord asked as they got moving again.

Roper grinned. 'Collect that thousand dollars for a start, then ride along until tomorrow morning in case you need an extra gun against those Indians crowding the hills. After that I aim to make a stop over in Wichita.'

McCord pulled out from the inside pocket of his buckskin coat a wad of bills that would have choked a cow. He peeled off ten and handed them over to the surprised Roper. 'If Grant didn't die from that shot you fired, the next time I see you I'll want that dinero back, so don't go spending it in Wichita.'

The bloodlust started to rise as Roper stared across at McCord. It cooled as he felt the full mesmeric quality of the cold, black eyes, and he stifled back the hot reply that was on his tongue. 'I've got plenty of my own dinero to spend in Wichita, and what's more, if I only had a dollar when I arrived there, I'd have me a good time and leave with a fistful.'

McCord nodded, but his expression did not relax any. He realised that Roper had accepted him as having the edge in a confrontation, so he decided to use him, and at the same time keep him around until he was sure that Grant was dead.

'Well, a man can never gather too much dinero,' he said. 'In fact we're going to help ourselves to plenty pretty soon. If you're interested in a share, we'll cut you in.' Mordant threw a doubtful look at his chief, but he kept his own counsel.

Roper took a long time replying but at

length he made up his mind. 'You can count me in. Just one thing though, it don't alter the fact that I'm heading first to Wichita. I've got things to do that won't wait. I guess a day there will do, then I'll catch up.'

McCord nodded assent. If Roper didn't show up in three or four days then he would know that Grant was still alive and had exacted revenge.

Things happened too fast for Amos. It took too long for him to realise that Roper was clinging to the horse Indian fashion. As the animal passed the thicket of mesquite and Amos' first glance, as he rode out from cover, mistakenly took in a riderless horse. He darted a look behind to the trail, then his heart jumped with alarm as Roper's gun fired. He saw Steve pitch from the saddle, and was caught in indecision. He fired a couple of despairing shots at the horseman, then slid from the saddle to check on Steve.

Blood was pouring down Steve's face, and tears of anguish filled the blackman's eyes as he looked for signs of life, but Steve was inert, lying like a sack of grain where he had fallen. Amos was so concerned that he failed to see the Indians moving down the hillside, and when he knelt beside Steve to inspect the wound he was unaware of their arrival on the trail. He looked up quickly, more in surprise than alarm, as the leader came

alongside and dropped to his knees beside
him. The Indian gave a reassuring sign to
Amos and leaned over Steve to inspect the
wound. He slipped Steve's bandanna from
his neck and wiped the blood away, showing
a furrow alongside the temple. The furrow
rapidly filled with blood again, and the
Indian took time feeling for heartbeats.

The tension left the Indian's face as he
pointed to Amos' bandanna and held out a
hand for it. Quickly he made a pad which he
pressed on the wound, then wound Steve's
own bandanna around the head to keep the
pad in place. He barked orders at the dozen
other Indians gathered close, then held
Amos' arm, pointed to Steve, nodded, then
made a big play of breathing in and out. The
blackman's relief welled up in him, and his
face split in the big, crooked grin his scars
created. He reached out involuntarily,
clasped the Indian's hand and pumped it
enthusiastically.

'I'm Sequoia,' the Indian said, his face
again impassive. 'And you are Amos?' The
blackman nodded, his eyes mirroring surprise. 'Lone Bear told me the name of the
man who was with Steve at Lone Bear's
camp.'

The other Indians had ridden back up the
hill but Sequoia dropped to the ground
beside Steve again, and laid him in a more
comfortable position, then he nursed

108

Steve's head with a tenderness that proved to Amos the real depth of friendship that existed between the redskin and whiteman.

At length, a couple of Indians returned, bringing a travois. Between them, they strapped Steve on, and set off back up the hill. Sequoia sprang astride his horse, reached for the lead rein of Steve's mount, and indicated with a glance to Amos to follow them. Then slowly, so that the travois would travel smoothly, they rode up the hillside.

They topped one ridge where the ground dropped away a little before stretching out towards a further ascent to the top, and here they were joined by another hundred or so braves. At the top of the next rise they were probably a thousand feet higher than the trail, and the top flattened out into a wide plain. Here more braves joined them, leaving some along the ridge as sentries, and by the time Sequoia called a halt, there must have been all of five hundred Indians flanking their leader and the carefully-drawn travois.

Tepees appeared, sprouting like magic out of the earth, and they unstrapped Steve out of the travois and carried him into a tepee. Sequoia waved Amos forward to join him, then a squat, older Indian brought some articles and dropping alongside Steve, took away the bandannas. He checked the wound, probing each side of it with long, lean fingers, then he picked up a couple of pieces of bark, with resin glistening in globules on them and placed them carefully on the wound, keeping them in place with a leather headband. He then poured some green liquid into a clay bowl from a leather container, trickling the liquid drop by drop into Steve's mouth.

It took no more than ten minutes after the libation for Steve to show signs of recovery. His breathing, which had been so shallow, improved so that the rise and fall of his chest was apparent to the delighted Amos.

The Indian appeared satisfied and before leaving the tepee gestured to Amos to follow him. Outside, Sequoia took a seat beside a fire which was just bursting into life, and invited Amos to sit with him. Then in slow, halting English, he elicited from Amos all that had transpired since Lone Bear and his braves had taken sides against Sergeant Hook and his men.

They ate a meal of maize-cake and pemmican, washed down with water, and all the time Sequoia kept Amos talking, adding to his knowledge of the white man's tongue. Since his acquisition of a smattering of the strange language Steve had taught him, Sequoia had concluded that in the long run, facility with the language for negotiation would serve his tribe better than all the guns and arrows. History would prove that Sequoia did more for the Indian Nation with his silver tongue than the rabid warmongers who decimated their numbers by ill-advised uprisings and hastily conceived battle plans.

Many times throughout the day, Sequoia and Amos checked on Steve's progress, but it wasn't much before sunset when their visit coincided with his return to consciousness. When they stood beside him his eyelids flickered, then stayed open. He stared curiously at the skin sides of the tepee, as his mind tried to adjust, then he saw Amos, struggled with recognition, then returned the man's wide smile with a weak grin. Then his eyes fastened on the Indian's face, and his eyes widened with surprise and pleasure. He tried to get up, but the pain in his head made him sink back down, but he held out his hand in welcome.

Sequoia went down on one knee and took Steve's hand and wrist in both hands. 'It makes Sequoia glad to see the light in your eyes again,' he said soberly, and Steve grinned again.

'It's good to see you again, Sequoia,' Steve felt the seat of his wound very carefully and winced. Memory came flooding back. He remembered Roper flashing past alongside the mesquite bush, then the gunflash from beneath the neck of the man's horse. 'What happened?' he asked.

'That polecat shot you, then rode off the trail to the east, and just after I got to you

111

Sequoia and his men showed up. I guess they took over from there.'

'That rider joined the six wagons travelling north,' the Indian said. 'Lone Bear said the men you fought when you met him came from those wagons.'

Steve considered things a bit before replying. 'So Roper's met up with McCord.' Then he went on to explain to Sequoia all about McCord and his crew of Union soldiers. Sequoia digested the information, but whilst he understood Steve's strong feelings, he himself could not raise much rancour against McCord's men; after all, they'd only been killing and pillaging whites. The name McCord gave him food for thought however, and when Steve told him that McCord would be heading north on a seven-day journey to where he had hidden all the valuables he had stolen, Sequoia remembered and nodded his head with satisfaction.

'It is good. The Sioux and Cheyenne will be waiting for him. I will pass the word. Before the whitemen made war against each other McCord killed very many of their people, braves, women and children. He brought firewater for the braves, and when they slept from firewater, he came back to their villages and killed everyone. The last time, Ogalla, son of Tetuan, one of the big Sioux chiefs, was left for dead, but he did not die, and swore vengeance. So McCord's name is known to all Plains Indians. You must let them travel north, and not fight. Too many men against two. If you meet Ogalla you will find he speaks your tongue like you. His mother, Tetuan's squaw, is white.'

'There were fifteen more men when I saw them down south,' Steve replied, amplifying with his fingers the number fifteen. 'So we could leave the rest to Ogalla, but we'll follow them, just in case.'

Sequoia sat back on his haunches, and contemplated his friend. He had understood most of Steve's words but the sign language had filled in the omissions. A smile played on his lips as he reasoned that if Steve kept up the rate of attrition, Ogalla would be lucky to find the object of his vengeance intact.

With the knowledge that the fight could be taken out of his hands, Steve remembered the long, low wagon, so he told Sequoia about the guns that fired faster than a man could blink, and the Indian nodded, saying Ogalla would be warned.

The effects of the concussion Steve had suffered wore off rapidly, and within the hour from regaining consciousness he was on his feet, improving every minute.

With his improvement came the beginnings of a nagging worry about Jill Rankin. Obviously the Stage-coach had carried on, driver and passengers unaware of what had happened backtrail, and that meant Jill would be in danger if Roper elected to leave the safety of McCord's wagon-train. He finally decided that Roper's anger had been against him, not Jill, and as far as the man knew, he was now dead. So he decided to set out at sun-up.

The old Indian took another look at Steve's wound, and nodded happily as he replaced the first pieces of bark with two more, even more heavily laced with resin. He said a few words to Sequoia as he left the tepee and the young son of Chief Bald Eagle turned to Steve. 'You understood?' he questioned, and Steve nodded carefully.

'Yeah. He said not to take it from the wound until the full moon,' he replied.

Sequoia smiled his delight. 'You don't forget our tongue, Steve. I'm glad, because I think of your tongue all the time.'

'When I get back home, I'll bring you books,' Steve said. 'I'll show you how to learn from books.' He held up his hands and counted off six fingers. 'The sixth full moon I'll see you where we first met. Amos too, if he'd like.'

The Indian's eyes lit with pleasure, and he clasped Steve's hand first, then Amos', to seal the bond. Amos' smile was wider than usual; he liked the tall, dignified young Indian, and felt proud to be classed a friend.

He turned to Steve, and his face was serious. 'I'd be mighty pleased to come with you, Mister Steve,' he said.

NINE

Jill Rankin spent the rest of the day staring out of the windows looking for sight of Steve. It was hot and uncomfortable in the coach, and dust cast up by the team found its way inside. She was not prepared to admit as much to herself, but she would not have noticed the discomforts if Steve had been in view.

The hour rest she had at Chiksaw where Jack Bennett pulled in for a team change and a meal did nothing for Jill's mood. Indeed, when she asked Jack Bennett about Steve and Amos, his reply increased her feeling of anger.

'I reckon they've stopped by to pay a visit to some of their Injun friends. I guess they'll show up in Wichita in a couple of days.'

She had nodded, her face stiffly composed in an attempt not to show her feelings, but she felt resentment. It was fine for Steve to be on friendly terms with Indians, she thought, but for her part all Indians looked the same, all hostile. She should have refused to return to Wichita. Her brow blackened as she worked out that by now she would only have been a week away from Waco.

It was well after sun-down when Jack Bennett drove along Main Street and dropped her off at her aunt's place, which turned out to be the clothing shop, just off the middle of Main Street.

Martha Howe, a buxom, motherly soul, had run the clothing shop for ten years or so, a venture she had started more to fill in her time than for profit. Her husband, Neil, was away more time than he spent at home, travelling the outlying ranches with his blacksmith's gear fastened to a burro. Once a week, he attended his smithy at Wichita, and in all, he made a good living.

Jill was immediately gathered into Mrs Howe's embrace and flooded with questions intended to amplify the bald telegraph Steve had forwarded from Enid.

Between answering the questions and making inroads into the meal her aunt put in front of her, Jill temporarily forgot her anger at Steve's desertion. It was only when she lay awake in her own bed, and Steve's image floated in front of her mind's eye, that she allowed the rancour to take over. She determined to ride out first thing in the morning so that she could vent her spleen at the earliest possible moment. Before sleep claimed her, however, she was aware only

116

that she wanted to see him.

Contrary to her intention, she slept long after sun-up, and when she finally left Wichita astride her handsome, paint mare, it only needed a couple of hours to mid-day. The mare, revelling in the freedom of the open range, stretched her stride and Jill felt elated with the pure pleasure of the ride.

With her mind on meeting Steve somewhere down-trail, she spared no glance to right nor left as she rode through a shallow canyon, and she failed to see the rider who topped the rim of a cutting that ran down to the canyon floor from the east. The rider however, was filled with unholy delight at the sight of her; and drawing his mount back from the rim spurred the animal into a quick run below the rim, along the breast of the hill to arrive at the canyon's end before the girl. When the paint emerged from the canyon, Roper sat his mount in the middle of the trail, his six-guns levelled at the on-coming horse.

Jill stared aghast at the rider whose intent was plain for anyone to see. She hauled her mount to a stop. 'Get out of my way, Mister! I've nothing to say to you!' Jill snarled.

Roper laughed. 'Oh no, ma'am! You don't escape me this time! And there's nobody going to save your hide either. That hombre Grant'll help nobody any more. We met up yesterday, and he ended up with a bullet in his head.'

The blood drained from Jill's face and she stared in horror at Roper. When she remembered her mood of yesterday when she had believed Steve had deserted her to her discomfort, a feeling of utter desolation flooded her, and she knew she would have to help herself.

Anger rose up in her, as the mocking Roper seemed to register every nuance of evil possible, and she reached for the little Derringer she kept tucked in her belt. Her hand clasped the butt, drawing it free, and as she levelled it Roper fired with cold deliberation.

When Jill fired she was in mid-air as the paint mare dropped dead with a bullet in her heart. Jill thudded to the ground, and the Derringer landed almost at the feet of Roper who had slid out of the saddle. He picked it up nonchalantly and reached down, grasped the collar of her blouse and jacket and hauled her to her feet, his wolfish smile bringing her to immediate awareness of her danger.

With his free hand he reached for her blouse and ripped it from top to bottom, then with deliberate savagery he did the same to her petticoat, baring her firm, white breasts to his evil stare.

Fury made Jill fight, squirm and kick, but Roper was strong and determined. The hours in the Stage-coach under the restraint of her gun, and Grant's intervention at Enid, made him determined to possess her, and her struggles and entreaties only made him more resolved. He hit her a stunning blow on the side of the chin, then dragged her unconscious body and slung her over the saddle pommel; then, climbing into the saddle, rode away off the trail to the east.

'Did you hear that, Amos?' Steve asked. 'Sounded like two shots.'

'Yeah, that was two shots sure enough,' Amos replied.

'Let's take a look then!' Steve barked, and he increased Apache's speed along the breast of the curving mountain. Amos urged his grey to keep pace.

Five minutes later they overlooked the trail, where it entered the long canyon before the last lap to Wichita, and even at the distance they guessed the inert bulk on the trail was a dead or badly injured horse. Another five minutes brought them to where Jill's paint lay in premature death.

Steve studied the trail carefully. He saw where the paint's rider had hit the ground. The deep imprint told him that either a slim, small man had lain there or a woman. The hoofprints of the other rider's horse were deeper leaving the trail than upon arrival, so the horse was carrying two when it left.

'C'mon Amos, there's been some devilry

here, we'll follow the cayuse that headed off the trail.'

They breasted the rim of a fold that ran almost level with another larger hill huddling the foot of the mountain that glowered over the surrounding plain. At the same time both men saw the horse with its double burden, halfway up the next hill. Amos pointed and shouted but Steve was already waving him on.

Steve allowed Amos to get level, and yelled to be heard above the wind. 'Keep following him, Amos, let him see you, but don't get too close. I'm going to ride wide.'

Amos waved his acknowledgment, and Steve gave his mount its head, veering to the left. The stallion fairly flew over the ground to the rise of the next hill, then scrambled across the hill's face like a mountain goat.

Steve gained the top of the hill, and his all-embracing glance took in a large herd some miles away to the east at the foot of the mountain, and farther away, six moving dots which he took to be wagons, and just below him, a horse emerged from a cleft in the hill with a rider he immediately recognised as Roper. The apparently unconscious form in front of Roper was face down, but that it was a woman he had no doubt.

Just before Roper reached the bottom of the hill, his passenger must have regained consciousness. Steve saw the woman lift her knees to press the horse's shoulder, then keeping her head down to slide under the reins, pushed hard. She fell heavily to the ground, rolled a few times, then lay still. Roper cursed and struggled to haul his mount around. He saw Steve at the same moment that Steve recognised Jill.

There was blood on her face, where she had grazed a thorn in falling, and Steve's concern made him lose concentration. He unsettled Apache by his quick turn in the saddle to take a better look at the girl; the stallion stumbled and fell heavily, throwing Steve out of the saddle. Roper was dismounted, six-guns flowing into his hands.

Steve fell with a thud and rolled a few times, Roper's eyes following him dispassionately, his right hand keeping in line with Steve's heart. Steve knew he should be going for his guns, but the jolt from his fall had returned the effects of his previous concussion. He rolled to a stop five yards away from the grinning Roper, and cursed his inability to help himself. Roper's aim was deliberate, and when the shot came, Steve could not understand why he felt no pain; then he saw Roper's expression change from savage glee to surprise, then vacuity, and Roper plunged face-first into the ground. Steve, scrambling to his knees, saw Amos riding downhill, his smoking rifle held aloft in triumph.

Jill was conscious when Roper fell, and she saw Steve climbing to his feet, and Amos bearing down upon them. She was suddenly aware of her torn clothing and she grabbed her jacket, pulling it as tightly around her as possible.

Steve got to her side. 'Thank heavens you're safe!' he said, then as Amos climbed down from his mount alongside them, 'Thank you, Amos! That was very good shooting.' Steve gripped the coloured man's arm fervently, and Amos smiled from ear to ear.

'I was lucky. The most I'd hoped for was to distract him until you were ready.' He turned to the girl. 'You all right, Miss Jill?'

'Yes, Amos, thanks to you both. He – shot my horse from under me, then knocked me unconscious.' The thought of her lovely paint mare now lying dead, brought tears flooding to her eyes, and in her haste to dash her tears away, she released the jacket she had held so tightly, leaving her bosom bare. Both men looked away, Steve to check on Apache, who had regained his feet, Amos to untie his saddle-roll, and spread out a blanket, which he proceeded to cut into with his knife.

Jill realised with sudden burning shame that she had left herself exposed to the men's gaze, and she clutched at the jacket again, her neck and cheeks aflame. The thought of

Steve's eyes upon her breasts made her hot and cold all over. Yet she experienced a strange, tingling excitement.

The emotions passed and Jill sat with her back to Amos, watching Steve as he dragged Roper's body alongside the bay stallion, then humped it over the saddle-pommel. He then collected Roper's lathered cayuse and took a couple of notches in the stirrup leathers to suit Jill. Then, as Steve led the animal up the grade, Amos dropped the garment he had fashioned out of the blanket in front of her.

Jill stared at it for a moment, then laughed delightedly. She turned and with eyes shining said, 'Oh, Amos! You're wonderful. Now why didn't I think of that? Thank you!'

'Aw, it's nothing,' Amos murmured happily, as Jill looked again at Amos' handiwork.

He had cut a hole for her head in the centre of the blanket, two smaller holes in line each side of the larger hole, then a circular cut two and a half feet from the centre of the neck-hole, completing a garment that would adequately serve to cover her embarrassment.

Jill walked a little way up the hill, and with her back to the two men, rapidly donned the rough-made blouse, and covered it with her jacket. When she rejoined Steve and Amos she had completely recovered her poise.

'Thank you both,' she said. 'You saved me from a lot of trouble. There's no doubt you saved my life.'

Amos shuffled his feet and just grinned, while Steve shrugged, removed his sombrero and dusted himself down with it, revealing the leather head-band that kept the resin-coated bark in place. Jill stared at it and, pointing to the bark dressing, said, 'He – he said you were dead, that he had shot you yesterday. Did he do that?'

Steve smiled at her expression of concern. 'Yes, I guess he had me cold today too.'

'Just how did you come to my help?' Jill asked.

'We heard two shots, and we got all the answers at the mouth of the canyon. So it was only a matter of following the trail. One shot killed your cayuse. Did you fire the other?'

Jill nodded. 'Yes, but I lost the Derringer when I fell.'

Steve crossed to the corpse and searched the jacket, finding the gun in an inside pocket; he checked it, then handed it over to the girl, who watched him with an expression of tenderness that Steve had never seen before, and for the first time he felt tongue-tied and stumble-footed.

'We'd better be getting back to Wichita,' he managed after hemming and hawing a couple of times.

As they climbed into their saddles, and Steve led the way up the hill, Jill considered his back view, and consciously admitted to herself that she was very much taken with the young owner of the store her father managed. Steve for his part, remembering her tender expression, found strange emotions temporarily taking over.

Gaining the top of the hill, he thrust these thoughts away and turned to study the terrain again. The dust cloud that hung over the large herd had moved on a piece to the north, but McCord's wagons were all lost under the merest puff of dust in the distance. He pointed to the nearest dust pall.

'See there, Amos! That's a mighty big herd, and McCord's wagons are no more than ten miles ahead of them.' Amos and Jill followed the direction of Steve's pointing finger. 'In about three days I reckon McCord will kill every last trail-herder and run that herd into Topeka. Unless we take a hand!'

Jill's eyes rounded in surprise, she looked at Amos who was nodding in agreement, his expression serious. 'So that's the business you have to get done before you take me to Waco?' she blurted. 'Who's this McCord? and whose herd is that?'

'It's a long story, Jill, and the best man to tell it is Amos.' Having said that, Steve started Apache on the move again, leaving Jill and Amos to ride together, and before

125

they reached Wichita, Amos had recounted all he knew about Sheridan's Light Horse, and Steve's part in the revenge to date.

TEN

'That's a prime herd right enough,' Mordant remarked, as he reined his mount to McCord's slower pace. 'I reckon we can take 'em without much trouble. I made out twenty-five riders and two wagons.'

McCord received Mordant's report with his customary curt nod. 'We'll take 'em when we want. Do you reckon they know we're ahead of them?'

'I didn't see any scouts far enough ahead to get us in their sights, but no doubt the riders on point have seen our trail. I guess if we were worrying them any, their scouts would have caught up to give us a closer look.'

'Yes, I'm sure you're right. Well, we'll get them into Topeka inside three days, it won't matter if we hustle 'em a bit.'

'Five thousand head are going to take some handling,' Mordant said. 'We'll need every last man until we get them through the pens at Topeka.'

'I don't agree!' McCord snapped. 'Those herders have been on the trail for maybe two or three months, and they've needed to be about thirty strong, but for a two-day chore ten good men are enough.'

Mordant digested this in silence, he also considered the rest of the men. It would be better to end up at Topeka with men who had never been to the Nebraska cache, and he dredged his memory to remember those who had made the run. There were just four, Zeke Rance, Lobo Dean, Eb Faulkner and Sam Stuckey. They had ridden with Sheridan's Light Horse almost from the beginning, and each was as evil a double-dyed villain as the next. They had stuck with McCord for the profit at the end of the road, but they would have no compunction in slitting his throat at the first sign of treachery.

Mordant toyed with feeding the information to Eb Faulkner, who could be trusted to treat the news with quiet calm. Further consideration brought back Mordant's natural caution. There was something about Faulkner that steadied him, a cold implacability, and an ability to keep his own counsel that equalled even McCord's. One reference to manipulated depletion of manpower as a matter of policy could well be taken by Faulkner as the excuse to run his own show, sounding the death knell for both officers. He would have to make darned sure that Faulkner and his cronies went under.

Wichita lay just in front of them and Steve pulled his mount to a stop. Jill and Amos followed suit and waited for the reason.

'I've got to tote the corpse to the Sheriff,' Steve said. 'There's no reason for you to be there, Jill, so Amos will see you home. We'll see you in the morning to let you know our plans.'

'No!' Jill said sharply. 'We've got room enough. Amos will stay and you can join us after you have seen the Sheriff.'

Steve was about to expostulate but seeing Jill's expression thought better of it. 'When my aunt and uncle know what you've done for me today, they wouldn't take kindly to you staying anywhere else,' she continued.

Steve shrugged his shoulders deprecatingly. 'We haven't done any more than anyone else would do, given the chance to be at the same place at the same time. However, I'll wait here until you've made it into town.'

Amos nodded, and set his grey towards Wichita, and Jill, after a long look at Steve, gigged her tired mount in Amos' wake.

Steve gave them ten minutes to clear Main Street; then he rode into Wichita, pulling up alongside the jail-house, where a shingle told him Walter Rutter was the Sheriff. Tying Apache with his burden to the hitch-rail, Steve climbed the steps and knocked at the door.

Sheriff Rutter, a thin, gangling man, with

a long sallow face, dark hair and mournful expression, was just buckling his gunbelt around him. He looked up at Steve out of bird-bright, black eyes.

'What's your trouble, Mister?' he asked. 'Make it quick, anyways; I'm on my way to find out what's happened to a girl that had her cayuse shot from under her, then disappeared.'

The surprise showed on Steve's face. He hadn't expected the Sheriff to know of the attack on Jill. 'I guess I can save you the journey then, Sheriff. If the girl is Jill Rankin, riding a paint mare, then she got home just ahead of me. I've got the hombre that killed her cayuse draped over my bronc outside. Hombre called Roper, my pard and me caught up with him after reading the sign where her horse got killed.'

Rutter was a good listener, and making no comment, crossed to the door, and took a couple of paces to the sidewalk rail. Only a glance sufficed and he was back inside the office. 'That's Roper right enough,' he said. 'And there just ain't nobody who's going to be sorry. He's passed through Wichita often enough.' He paused. 'I didn't get to know your moniker, Mister.'

'The name's Grant, Steve Grant. I'm from Waco, and I own the store there, where Miss Jill's father is the manager.'

Rutter nodded, then crossed to the table

129

and made a note of what Steve had said, then turned back to Steve, a friendly light in his eyes. 'We're all obliged to you, Grant. Moss Tynan, of the Triple Circle ranch, came in about twenty minutes ago, he had dragged the paint off the trail, and brought the gear in he'd stripped from the dead horse.' He nodded to a door behind him. 'It's out there when Miss Jill wants it. Moss and the others are waiting over at the "Traveller" for me to take 'em searching for the girl. You want to come over and meet 'em?'

'No. I reckon not. I just want to get rid of the cadaver, then I'll be calling on the Howes.'

They left the jailhouse and a crowd had assembled on the sidewalk to inspect Roper's remains. He hadn't been much in life, and judging by the speed individuals moved on, he palled as a spectacle in death. Rutter stayed four men by calling their names, then turned to Steve. 'Get him cut down, Grant, and they'll take him to the funeral parlour.'

Steve complied, then, remembering Jill's directions, rode along Main Street to the turning that led to Neil Howe's smithy. When he reached the yard, Jill came from the house to greet him, followed by her uncle, who had returned from the north trail just after Jill had left.

Neil Howe, a dark, handsome giant, shook the younger man's hand warmly as Jill made the introductions. He liked what he saw. 'Mighty pleased to meet you, Steve, and I guess we're thankful for what you and Amos have done for Jill.'

Steve glanced towards Jill and again found her with a velvet-soft expression in her eyes; he switched his gaze back to Neil Howe.

'Amos and I were happy to be at the right place at the right time, Mr Howe,' he said simply. 'And I hope we'll be no inconvenience to you here until tomorrow.'

'Glad for your company,' Howe replied heartily.

Steve nodded, a smile of contentment on his face, then he led Apache towards the box Howe indicated, followed by Jill who seemed determined not to let him out of her sight.

'That's sure some hunk of horseflesh, Steve,' Howe said, when the stallion was in his box. 'Where did you get him?'

'Saw him as a foal down on the Neuces,' Steve replied. 'And near enough hand-reared him. Only thing is, he won't have anyone else handle him.'

'He's a beautiful animal,' Jill said at length. 'I'm sure he and I will get along when we know each other a little better.'

Steve glanced back at her, and received a very direct look, that inferred she would be around to get on good terms with his horse, and a feeling from deep down told him he would never be at peace again unless she was within calling distance.

When at length Apache had his head in the manger champing contentedly at a mixture of oats and hay, they walked back to the house, ready for anything Mrs Howe would provide.

During the evening, Steve let it be known that he and Amos would be staying only one night, and when Neil Howe and his wife expressed disappointment, he felt constrained to explain the reason why. When now and again he glanced towards Jill, he found a very speculative look on her face.

Just before Jill retired for the night she expressed the thoughts that had been chasing around in her mind. 'I don't see it's any fight of yours, saving that herd from McCord. I go along with warning the drovers, but there's no sense risking your lives alongside men you know nothing of. They might themselves have stolen the herd downtrail.'

Steve looked at the girl, sharp surprise in his eyes, then a slow smile spread across his face. 'That possibility never crossed my mind,' he admitted. 'You sure could be right though. Yes, I guess we'll catch up with them at speed so they'll have the best time to organize a welcoming party when McCord moves in.'

'Well! Now that's settled, there's no reason why I can't ride along,' Jill stated firmly.

'Uh – hold on there!' Steve expostulated. 'Whether we take a hand or not, we won't be heading back this way until we've followed McCord to the bitter end, and that could mean Topeka, and then Nebraska.'

'And you think I'd be in the way. Is that it?' Jill asked, her face now taut. Then when Steve made no immediate response she continued in a very level voice. 'I'll tell you once only, Steve Grant, I can handle six-guns and rifle as well as most men.'

Steve flashed a quick look at Neil Howe, who shrugged his shoulders expressively, passing the decision back to Steve. 'There are more than twenty cold-blooded killers following McCord's orders,' he said quietly. 'Men who have lived the past four or five years steeped in the blood of innocents; there's no call for you to risk everything tangling with such trash.'

'There's as much reason for me as you and Amos, Steve Grant! More perhaps, seeing that most of their victims were women.'

If she expected Steve to concede then she was disappointed, and when Jill finally made her way to bed, he still had not agreed for her to travel.

Sleep did not come easily to either of them that night. Jill, fuming over the possibility that in the end Steve would not agree to her accompanying Amos and himself, and Steve, weighing up the dangers against his heartfelt

133

desire to have Jill alongside him. When sleep eventually took over, neither had resolved anything.

It was upon awakening that Steve came up with the answer. He and Amos were so heavily outnumbered that they would in any case have to continue a sniping war of attrition against McCord's hoodlums, so Jill should not be placed in any immediate danger, and at length he was able to square his desire for her company with his belief that he and Amos could protect her.

When he finally went downstairs his first glance at Jill confirmed his belief he'd have had trouble from her if he had made any other decision. She was dressed in range clothes, short jacket, rough woollen shirt, levis, leather chaps, calf-length boots, and twin, pearl-handled .45's hung from her belt. She was placing a well-oiled Remington repeater back in its wall-holder as Steve entered the room. Despite himself, Steve could not restrain a wide smile.

'I see you're all set then,' he remarked conversationally. 'You're toting enough hardware to start a range war.'

'Now you're mocking me, Mister Steve Grant,' Jill said with some asperity. 'I hope I don't have cause to prove anything, but should I have to, then you'll find I'm not wearing this armoury for decoration.'

'Yeah, and you can believe her, young

feller,' Neil Howe put in. 'I'm giving you a couple of spare horses to take along. You can use 'em to tote along provisions we've got ready.'

'That's mighty good of you,' Steve replied. 'And I hope it won't be too long before they're back in your stables.'

Neil Howe smiled away Steve's gratitude as Amos preceded Martha Howe into the room, bearing huge serving plates covered with bacon, eggs and kidneys. Martha set down plates of fried potato rounds, then returned to the kitchen for homemade bread and coffee.

Amos looked from Steve to Jill and, rightly interpreting the situation, he allowed his customary smile to split his expressive face.

It needed about three hours to sundown when they topped a rise and saw the rippling sea of muscle, bone and prime beef that moved slowly across the wide prairie under the guidance of herders who had stayed alongside their charges for close on three months. They were moving so slowly, they hardly stirred the dust, and Steve reckoned they would soon be bedding down for the night.

'We'll ride around 'em wide,' Steve said as Jill and Amos pulled up beside him. 'I reckon they'll be milling them before much longer, as we'll pass on our news before they all gather for chow.' His sidelong glance at Jill took in the fact that she still looked as fresh as paint after a long day under the hot sun. Her eyes were alert as she caught his glance.

'Fine-looking herd,' she said. Steve took her remark to mean well-disciplined; they were still too far away to take account of the condition of the animals. He grunted agreement, and gigged Apache forward again.

Twenty minutes later, they rode in just ahead of where the herd stood cropping at the bunch grass which grew in plentiful supply. The chuck-wagon stood well back from the herd, and a couple of men were manhandling a stove from the low tailboard. Two men sat their horses near the chuck-wagon. Steve reined in and Jill and Amos pulled in right behind him.

'Howdye!' Steve volunteered. 'Who's running this herd?'

The two men appraised the newcomer. Both were range-hardened men with lean, clear-cut features. One was dark-haired and the other blond, their eyes bright with interest. Steve reckoned them both to be in their late thirties.

'We do. And who wants to know?' the dark-haired one asked.

'The name's Grant. Steve Grant. The lady is Miss Rankin and my pard's moniker is Amos. We've got some news for you that you'd better believe.'

Both men tipped their hats to Jill then

136

turned their attention to Steve.

'The name's Jim Calder,' the dark-haired man said. 'And my pard's Dan Holt. We've brought this herd from Langtry down on the Pecos river.'

'That's sure some drive, Mr Calder,' Steve replied. 'I guess you'll be glad when you can trade at Galveston again.'

Calder gave a short laugh and nodded, but Holt shrugged. 'I guess it'll be a long time before selling steers for trans-shipment up the Mississippi will show a worthwhile profit. So I reckon we'll do this trip a few more times.' Then when Steve nodded his agreement, 'How about this news? Why don't you climb down off those broncs, and tell us while we wait for the cook to get the coffee brewing?'

Steve slid out of the saddle and Jill, Amos and the two men followed suit, ground-hitching their mounts.

'We won't be staying long,' Steve said decisively. 'And the sooner you know what we've got to say the better, so this is it. Just ahead of you there are about twenty-five ex-troopers who intend to win themselves a herd between here and Topeka.'

Jim Calder and Dan Holt were immediately all attention, and waited for Steve to continue.

'We've tracked 'em clear from Waco, and I've had a couple of runs-in with the boss man, Tim McCord, and I can tell you he and his men will kill just for the heck of it, so you don't treat 'em lightly. They've got one wagon carrying five or six machine-guns that fire faster than a man can blink. I guess they've got your herd earmarked to take over.'

'Bill Carter, our scout, reported having picked up wagon tracks and about sixteen ridden broncs. They're running a cavvy of spare horses too.' Calder spoke slowly. He stared at Steve then said deliberately, 'You ain't one of them are you, son? Aiming to scare us into giving up the herd without a fight?'

'Nope, siree!' Steve snapped. 'No matter what happens to you and your beeves, I intend trailing every last one of those coyotes until they're dead. I'm just pointing out their intentions. You can stay and fight if you want, or when they show their hand, ride into Topeka ahead of them with docu-mentary evidence of ownership, that way you should have the backing of the law.'

'Well, most of this herd carry our brands,' Dan Holt growled. 'But there's no way we'll depend upon some lawman to sort out our troubles. Nope, we're obliged to you for the warning, and we'll have eyes on McCord's gang muy pronto, so if and when he attacks he'll get a mighty hot reception.'

'If that's your decision, Mr Holt, I wish

you the best of luck. I suggest though, you let your men know exactly what sort of a fight they'll be into if McCord attacks.'

'Yeah. We'll tell 'em,' Calder interposed. 'They've all got shares in this herd above their forty and found, so no matter what sort of a fight crops up, they'll be in it.'

There didn't seem to be anything more to say, so Steve just nodded and changed the subject. 'Well, I guess we'll be glad to share that brew of coffee before we move on.'

'Sure thing, Grant,' Calder answered, and he and Dan Holt crossed to the chuck-wagon to collect some boxes which they ranged around as seats. 'There you are, ma'am,' Calder said to Jill. 'Make yourself comfortable, the coffee should be ready in about ten minutes.'

Steve and Amos sat with Jill in the middle, relaxed and contented while the herd settled and riders started to come in to the chuck-wagon. Most of the riders turned to scrutinize the newcomers, and more than one eye lingered on Jill, but in no way to give offence.

Three men who had been in close conversation with Dan Holt, remounted their broncs and headed north-east, with the obvious intention of sighting McCord's outfit as soon as possible, and three more carried mugs over to the companions and struck up easy conversation during the time it took to drink the coffee. They spoke only in general terms about the drive from Pecos, and made no reference to the likely attack by McCord, which made Steve feel they were supremely confident.

A few minutes later Steve led Jill and Amos away to the north-west and the near-by hills, the thanks of the drovers in their ears.

ELEVEN

The sun had disappeared behind the hills, the wagons formed a tight circle, a line of picketed horses stood just outside the circle, and men drew in groups while they waited for the cook to come up with the evening meal. McCord and Mordant were sufficiently far away from the fire to keep their conversation private.

'So! This time tomorrow we take over the herd, eh?' Mordant asked casually. McCord's bleak eyes rested upon his lieutenant and a cold smile crossed his lips.

'No, I don't think so. We'll take 'em over at sun-up. Better to catch those herders with sleep in their eyes at sun-up than ready for action at sundown.'

Mordant was silent for a couple of minutes.

140

The thought of wet-nursing five thousand steers a day longer than he expected irked him, but finally he managed an expression of full accord as he realized that sundown tomorrow would see a considerable reduction in the number of shareholders in the Nebraska bonanza. 'Yeah!' he said at length, 'I like it.'

McCord's face showed that Mordant's approval was of little concern as he replied. 'Just make sure those machine-guns are in top order and every man's weapons are cleaned up ready. You'd better take over a machine-gun, and when the fight is won you can take care of the possible trouble makers.'

Mordant looked into McCord's basilisk eyes, and nodded, then he crossed to the chuck-wagon to collect two mugs of coffee. He returned to his seat after handing one mug to his chief. 'I'll see to things just as you say,' he said.

McCord took a gulp at the scalding coffee, then reached for a cheroot. 'Tell them we move out at three o'clock, I'll take care of the scouting to get us in the right position.'

There was no need for further talk and the two men sat smoking and drinking their coffee until the meal was ready. At three o'clock precisely McCord led his men south-west.

'What now?' Amos asked as he and Jill drew

abreast of Steve who had reined Apache in on the crest of the first foothill.

'Well, I don't think we'll have to worry too much about that herd. I believe McCord will get more than he expects from that quarter,' Steve replied. 'The way I see it, McCord will attack using just the low machine-gun wagon and riders, leaving the other wagons in the care of one or two men. It would be a bad blow to his ego if while he was attacking the herd we destroyed his wagons.'

'Now that's what I call a good idea!' Jill exclaimed. 'What are you going to do? Get close to them tomorrow?'

Steve shook his head. 'No, I think we've got to find McCord's camp tonight. I think that he will be moving in to attack at dawn. In his place that's what I would be doing.'

'So we keep on riding then?' Jill asked.

'Oh there's enough time for us to have a meal. Let's find a safe place.'

They rode across the shallow plateau to the next foothill, and an hour later settled down in a blind canyon where centuries of dribbling and cascading water had brought down enough dust to promote the plentiful growth of grass. Steve brushed down the horses while Amos and Jill got the fire going and prepared a meal.

Throughout the meal Steve was unusually quiet, so Jill and Amos left him to his thinking and kept up an amicable conversation until at length they cleaned up the utensils. Steve finally smoked his way through a cigarette then crossed to where Apache cropped contentedly, and saddled up.

Jill came alongside. 'Time to go then?' she asked.

'Time for me to go,' Steve replied. 'This is a good place for a temporary headquarters and there's no point in all of us leaving to do a chore that's as easily done by one.'

'Well, if that's what you want, Steve,' Jill said doubtfully.

'Yeah, that's what I want, because it makes sense. I'm hoping to be back before Mc-Cord attacks the herd.'

'You're right, Steve,' Amos put in quickly. 'Just take good care, I'll keep watch here.'

'We'll share the watch, Amos,' Jill stated, then as her hand rested briefly on Steve's arm, 'Yes, take care, Steve, we'll be waiting.'

Steve grasped her hand giving it some reassuring pressure, then patted Amos' shoulder. 'I'll give a couple of owl-hoots before riding in,' then he stepped lightly into the saddle and rode out beyond the firelight.

Jethroe Birch lay stretched full length no more than four hundred yards away from McCord's camp, keeping his eyes glued to the circle within the wagons as the light finally gave way to darkness. Eli Rich and Zeb Croker had left him to the chore of keeping tabs on McCord, while they returned to report to Calder and Holt. It was up to Birch to ride wide and fast to warn them if McCord made a move.

Before the light had faded, he had seen men busy cleaning and oiling sidearms and rifles, and there had been considerable activity around the long, low wagon that, according to Grant, carried some rapid-fire guns. With the coming of darkness only two men sat near the fire.

Eventually these last two men stood up, and headed towards one of the wagons. Later one man took a seat by the fire and threw some more timber on the blaze. The flames showed up the rifle he placed across his knees, and Birch decided everyone else had settled down to sleep.

Birch groaned inwardly. He knew now that he was in for a long wait. He pulled his slicker closer around himself, because with the sun's warmth gone, the wind took on a chill that seeped into the very marrow of one's bones. Characteristically, he fought down all thoughts of personal comfort, and taking a man-size bite from a thick plug of tobacco, he chewed himself into a good mood.

Hour followed hour until Jethroe Birch began to have doubts, then at last, the man who had kept the fire blazing stood up and collected various items from the chuck-wagon before ministering to a couple of pots hanging over the fire. About twenty minutes later, men were moving around within the circle.

Very little noise came from the camp as the men crowded around the fire, eating and drinking before heading for the deeper shadows that Birch knew to be the line of picketed horses. It was three o'clock when Birch saw the long, low wagon roll away from the circle into the night; and he heard the muffled hoofbeats as riders followed the wagon, headed south-west, and soon the only man left in camp was the cook, who had stood guard throughout the night.

Jethroe Birch eased himself away from the rim, stood up stiffly, and moved his limbs briskly to get the circulation going; then, returning to where his mount nodded in sleep, climbed into the saddle, and set off at an easy gait to the south. When he judged himself well out of earshot he gave the animal its head, travelling back to the herd without incident.

Steve rode for an hour and a half without being too concerned about other riders, being fairly sure that McCord would wish to take up a position against the drovers about half an hour before he planned to attack, which Steve expected to be at first light of day. From here on, however, he checked the stallion's speed and proceeded at a more cautious pace.

Later he drew his mount to a halt, hardly breathing as he listened, neither he nor the horse moving a muscle, then sure enough the creak of saddle-leather sounded close at hand. The rider had shifted in his saddle heavily enough to make the tell-tale noise, and Steve placed a warning hand on Apache's muzzle.

There was a whisper of sound amidst the prevailing noises of night as the horseman passed in a southerly direction, and Steve remained motionless for a few more minutes before continuing his journey. That the rider who had passed him was the scout for McCord's gang, Steve had no doubt, then about ten minutes later the ground trembled under him as something heavy passed by. He knew it to be the long, low wagon that carried the machine-guns. So his guess was right. McCord intended attacking at dawn, and with luck, Calder and Holt would be waiting.

Shortly afterwards Steve saw the camp fire where Zeke Rance sat surrounded by the five covered wagons. Steve stopped well out of the range of the firelight and, dismounting, led Apache wide of the camp, then inched his way back from the north. He slipped between two wagons and crossed stealthily, to stop behind the snoring man. He pressed the cold muzzle of his forty-five into the man's neck and waited for a reaction.

The man came awake quickly, and when he spoke his voice was level. 'Right, Mister. So you've got the drop. What now?'

'Drop the rifle and hold your hands high.'

Slowly the man obeyed, and Steve stepped back. 'Now turn around slowly.'

The man's face showed up, eyes glinting bitterly in the firelight, then they widened. 'You're Grant!' he exclaimed.

'Yeah, I never got around to knowing your handle,' replied Steve.

'Rance is the name, feller,' Zeke Rance said. 'So what do you do next?'

'I'm going to burn these wagons, haze away those cayuses, and feed you to the buzzards,' Steve replied flatly.

Rance took a quick intake of breath. Steve's bold assertion had him searching deep for courage. 'What in heck have you go against us, Grant? I never set eyes on you before we got to that blamed town down in Texas.'

'You're getting paid back for what you did in the war, Rance. You know what you did, and you know you can expect as little mercy as you showed to defenceless civilians.'

'I was a soldier, Grant! All I did was obey orders.'

'Yeah. And right now you're guarding the wagons you hoped to use to dispose of the booty you all stole in the war, while your pards have set out to steal a herd from men who have nursed the steers for the last three months. You're scum!'

As he spoke Steve holstered his gun and Rance ran his tongue around his lips nervously. 'You can lower your hands, Rance,' Steve said. 'Then draw. If you don't I'll kill you anyhow.'

Zeke Rance took a deep breath and slowly lowered his arms. Seconds ticked away, time loaded with gut-twisting apprehension for both men, then Rance went for his guns in a blur of movement.

The shots seemed simultaneous. Steve felt a tug as the bullet took a chuck out of his chaps, then watched as Zeke Rance clutched at his middle and toppled slowly to the ground.

Steve checked that Rance was indeed dead, then taking a blazing length of wood out of the fire, he set fire to every wagon. As the fire took hold he moved along the line of picketed horses, releasing them and hazing them away with shouts and slaps. When he was satisfied that every wagon was certain to burn to wood-ash he returned to his fidgeting horse, and headed at speed to the southeast.

Long before Tim McCord was able to pinpoint the herders' camp, Dan Holt, Eli Rich,

Zeb Croker and twelve other men were in position behind a deep fold in the nearby hill. In the camp, blankets piled around the fire gave the impression that at least twenty men lay deep in slumber, but the eight men left in camp were very much awake. If the attackers made the expected moves, then Jim Calder and his seven drovers reckoned that all-hell would be let loose at the base of the hill to the east before they would be drawn into the fracas. There were seven other men waiting at the southern side of the sleepy herd, ready to stampede the beasts to the north-east away from trouble.

Behind the fold in the hill, Dan Holt and Eli Rich were stretched out on the rim, their eyes glued to the flat land below, and their ears straining for any unusual sound. Zeb Croker, standing just below the rim, shifted his shoulder-bag to a more comfortable position. The bag contained a dozen primed and capped sticks of dynamite. Zeb had a nose for water, and his well-placed charges had often shown water to be where he had said, and herds had been saved. This time however, he had other plans for the dynamite.

With an hour to dawn, McCord's men moved into position just below the fold where Holt and his men waited. Whatever noise they made was lost in the soughing of the wind, but Eli Rich's nightsight was sharp enough to make out the darker shadows in the murk. He whispered the news to Holt and moved down to warn Zeb Croker, who in turn slid down the inside slope to warn the others.

Tim McCord soft-footed his way along the line of men, whispering his instructions to each little group. There were four machine-gunners on the low wagon with Mordant in command and Ken Rush the driver, nodding as he dozed. McCord prodded him, and pointing to the distant camp fire, told him to head north of the camp then to run south bringing all his guns to bear on the camp. One run, he told the driver, should kill every last man in the camp. The other riders would go straight into the camp when he had made his run.

Mordant said nothing as McCord gave him his instructions. He intended keeping a close eye on his superior when the ruckus started. Eb Faulkner, with his cronies Lobo Dean and Sam Stuckey grouped on the left-hand side of the machine-gun wagon, was quietly reflective. He had packed enough stores to last him a couple of weeks. If they looked like wiping out the herders quickly then he'd stay and collect his share at Topeka, but if things looked ugly he'd slide out and head for Nebraska.

McCord permitted himself a smile of satisfaction. He had previously instructed

Mordant to make Ken Rush, the driver, do a quick circling turn after the first attack so that their own riders in the camp would come under fire on the second run.

The double owl-hoot signal brought Jill to her feet and when Steve rode in she was immediately at his side, and the way she held his arm told him just how glad she was to see him back. His arm slipped around her shoulder naturally as he led her back to the fire. He felt her body shiver as the close contact reacted on her, and he was aware of his own excitement as he looked down at her lovely face in the firelight. He dragged his thoughts back to the urgent matters of the moment, and releasing his hold, he reached for a mug and filled it from the coffee pot suspended over the fire.

'Well! What happened?' Jill asked. She could still feel the pressure of his arm around her shoulders, and she felt the truth burst upon her. She loved Steve Grant, wholly and irrevocably, and she hoped that he would ultimately find he wanted her too with equal fervour.

Amos sat up as Jill posed the question and the big smile on his face showed his relief as he said, 'Glad to see you back, Mister Steve.'

Steve nodded his acknowledgment, then after telling them briefly all that had happened, made his intentions known. 'In about

151

an hour all Hades is going to start where that herd rests, and I've got to see what happens. I must know what McCord's got left when the fighting's done. You stay here, Jill, while Amos and I watch from the brow of the mountain.'

Jill swallowed her disappointment, and just nodded as she filled a mug with coffee for Amos, and while Amos sipped at the scalding liquid, Steve saddled up Amos' cayuse, and soon the two men rode out, leaving the girl alone.

TWELVE

The pards had barely settled on the skyline of the hill before the first grey tinge in the sky heralded the new day.

In the brief moment before all hell broke loose, four groups waited with bated breath for the first move. McCord's men for the word go, Dan Holt and Zeb Croker with his dynamite waiting for McCord's move, Jim Calder and his group in camp, under cover and ready to pick off those of the rustlers Dan Holt's men missed, and ready to set the herd in the right direction, Calder's segundo, Moss Kirk.

'Go!' McCord's command was muttered,

152

and barely reached the rim where Dan Holt and his men stood beside their mounts, but the word was followed by the rumble of the wagon taking off with a jerk, and the creaking of saddle-leather where men had climbed carelessly into their saddles. Then McCord's world fell apart.

Dan Holt's men came down the hill in a phalanx, their guns blazing, and Zeb Croker following unerringly the noise of the rumbling wagon, threw his first primed stick of dynamite. It landed plumb in the centre of the wagon, exploding with a blinding flash; fragmenting three machine-guns and their gunners, and sending a gun barrel flying to break Ken Rush, the driver's back. The next stick of dynamite shattered the back end of the wagon a split second after Mordant had dived to the ground, and the front end collapsed as the horses dragged it a few more desultory paces.

McCord's riders, caught in a hail of lead, galvanized their mounts into action in the hope of riding their way out of trouble, but unfortunately the light from the last explosion had shown up the pockets of horsemen and two more sticks of dynamite from Croker sent men and horses flying. Holt and the others started in to pick off the survivors.

McCord with the battle now in front of him, turned his mount without hesitation to the left and rode away fast along the base of the hill until he found a gully running up the side. Eb Faulkner had ridden off to the north at the first sign of ambush, and Mordant, still in one piece, came up off the ground, clawed Eli Rich who was passing, off his horse, and leaping astride, rode away Indian fashion, presenting no target. He rode north, hot on the trail of Eb Faulkner.

With the sun now clear, Mordant saw the rider ahead at the same time as Faulkner looked back. Faulkner reined his mount in, and waited gun in hand for the rider to catch up; he had a mocking grin on his face as Mordant pulled up.

'So, the brave officer ran away as well, eh?' he mocked.

'I left when there was no one else to fight, Faulkner,' snapped Mordant. 'I should shoot you for desertion.'

The smile left Faulkner's face and the ice came into his eyes. 'Just as well you think so, Mordant,' he said evenly, 'because you're going to have to try.' His hand moved into view as he spoke, showing the gun pointing at Mordant's heart.

Mordant's face was a study, and his blood turned to ice. He looked at Faulkner's sneering face, and he knew that death was a trigger pull away. All of Mordant's starch disappeared, and his face contorted as he started a blubbering entreaty for mercy.

Faulkner watched the man disintegrate

without one shred of pity, then with as much compunction as he would put down an injured cayuse, he fired a bullet into Mordant's heart, then after stripping the dead man's pockets, Faulkner remounted and turned to the north-west, in the general direction of Nebraska.

Tim McCord rode up the gully that led almost to the top of the hill, then across the face to the top. By the time daylight strengthened he was well on his way to the next higher chain of mountains. He was totally bemused at the ferocity and precision of the attack against him and his men. How in Hades had the drovers known of his intentions? And how had they been able to be exactly where they could wreak the most havoc in the shortest time? The element of surprise that shaken him to the roots, and his only concern for the moment was to get away and head for Nebraska.

Making the foot of the next mountain, he set his mount to the grade. Half the way up he turned into a gully that ran diagonally up the face of the mountain, then gave out as a canyon. He picked up the telltale marks of horses having been ridden in and out and, slipped from the saddle, took from his saddle-roll the hoof-muffles he always carried. Five minutes later he was back in the saddle and he kneed his mount forward as silently as a ghost.

McCord came upon the girl as she knelt at the trickling water, washing her face. He took in the three cayuses, one saddled up, the other two obviously due to carry the heavy packs beside the fire. The girl's jacket, hat and gunbelt lay on top of one of the packs. She stood up, wiping her face with the towel, then as she wiped she saw the rider who stared at her out of glittering eyes. Jill flashed a glance to where her gunbelt lay and McCord laughed unpleasantly.

'You'll never get there, lady,' he sneered.

'What do you want?' Jill asked.

McCord didn't answer immediately. Things clicked in his mind as he remembered Roper's words about the woman Grant was shepherding to Wichita. Roper had not returned, so Grant was not dead, and it was likely the woman standing in front of him was Grant's woman. Grant and his partner must have been dogging him all the time, and in some way were responsible for the disastrous dawn defeat.

'Just put your jacket and hat on, and get astride your cayuse. Make a play for the hardware and I'll leave you for buzzard meat.'

Steve and Amos stared down the hill in disbelief at the ferocity of the battle that had broken out. They saw figures like dolls fly in the flash of the first explosion, and the wagon break apart in the light of the next, then two further flashes of light from big explosions showed men and horses flying through the air. Guns continued to fire, but it seemed to the watchers that McCord's men were trying to escape from the massive onslaught, then Steve yelled, 'Look, Amos! The herd's stampeding!'

They watched the bawling cattle get into their lumbering stride. Distant firing fanned the animals' terror as they speeded up to a headlong rush.

The darkness slid away and they saw half-a-dozen riders race towards the northern end of the camp, attempting to escape from Holt and his men. The herd was in full flight, running north-east with drovers still firing, guiding them away from the camp. In the foreground, men and horses lay in death and the wagon lay in two grotesque halves. Three dead horses lay in their traces and three others stood fidgeting in their desire to get away.

They saw three of the escaping riders fall as the drovers in the camp opened up with their rifles. The other three turned sharply to the right and ran straight into a horrible death. The herd, now eating space, was upon them and thundered on, leaving men and horses a mutilated mass of broken bones.

There was nothing for Steve and Amos to

do but watch, and they saw the drovers now bringing the maddened herd under control.

'Let's take a look around, Amos,' said Steve at last, and they rode down to the scene of battle. There were ten corpses, and Steve was practically certain they had all been McCord's men, but neither McCord nor his lieutenant, Mordant, was amongst them.

At length they were joined by Jim Calder, Dan Holt and another drover, and Calder slapped Steve on the shoulder heartily. 'We've got to thank you, Grant, for your warning! I've no doubt you saved not only the herd, but our lives as well. If it hadn't been for Zeb Croker here, with his dynamite, we'd have had a tough fight anyway, and without your warning Zeb would never have had his sticks all primed up and ready.' He paused, then added, 'We all think you should be at Topeka when we sell the herd so that you can pick up shares.'

Steve smiled but shook his head. 'Thanks for the offer, but we'll just take a look at the other corpses so that we'll know just how many they've got left, then we'll be on our way.'

'There are six more dead men,' Holt put in. 'Three you're not going to piece together, the herd mangled them.'

'Any of your men bought it?' Steve asked.

'Four men with flesh wounds that won't worry them any,' Calder said, then continued, 'That's sixteen men they lost, maybe they left some in camp.'

'There was only one man left in camp,' Steve replied. 'He's dead and all the wagons are no more than heaps of ash. I saw to that after the party pulled out. So that leaves just three.'

The drovers gave Steve a long, respectful look, and Holt expressed what they all felt. 'Heck, Grant! I'd sure hate to have you tailing me.'

'He sure don't give up,' Amos put in flatly.

They rode to where the other three corpses lay, and Steve shook his head. 'McCord's not there, I reckon he got clear. He wouldn't have got caught up in that herd.'

'Do you want any help trailing him?' Calder asked.

Steve smiled his thanks, but shook his head. 'No, I know which way he'll be heading.' Then after shaking hands all round, Steve and Amos headed for the hills.

Just an hour or so later they rode into the canyon, ready for coffee and breakfast. They stopped beside the dying fire and looked at each other in dismay.

'She wouldn't have left her gunbelt behind,' Amos said.

'No. She wouldn't. Something has happened,' Steve replied. He fought down a momentary feeling of panic as he remembered three men had escaped the morning holocaust, and studied the floor of the canyon for sign. His face was serious when he reported his findings to Amos. 'A rider greased in with muffles on his horse's hooves. Must have taken her by surprise. It's my bet she left hand-tied, riding a led horse.'

'Let's go then!' Amos snarled.

'Hold on, Amos,' Steve remonstrated. 'We've got to eat a meal first, then we'll be in the right frame of mind to track her.'

'But anything could happen to her if we take too long in catching up!'

Steve shook his head. 'No. It would have happened here, Amos. Whoever has taken her is set on getting to some place else.'

Amos slid out of the saddle and threw wood on the fire, then undid one of the packs to get some food heated up. He glanced now and again at Steve, his expression doubtful. Steve had got over the shock and his mind was now working clearly.

'Look, Amos,' he said, 'We know that three men got away this morning. McCord, his second in command, Mordant, and another. Only one rider came this way. When he met up with Jill he might have found out about us. If the rider was McCord, he would have taken Jill to use her as insurance if and when we caught up with him.'

Amos lowered the coffee pot towards the newly-lit wood, and turned to look squarely into Steve's face. 'McCord, eh!' he exclaimed. 'If that man turns out to be Mc-Cord, I want to kill him with these.' He spread his massive hands to their full stretch.

'I understand the way you feel, Amos, but we may not have a choice how we kill him. We've just got to keep Jill alive.'

Amos made no reply. No matter what, Jill was the first consideration. They ate a quick meal, and with Steve reading the sign and Amos following with the two packhorses, they set off.

Tim McCord cleared the canyon and took to the rising ground, using every fold and gully to mask their movements from below. He was very conscious that in Steve Grant he had an implacable and deadly enemy, and he now blamed every reverse he had suffered all the way from Waco on the Texan. He felt for the first time in his life a niggling doubt that he would survive a confrontation. When he stopped to remove the mufflers from his mount, and to drape a blanket from the cantle of Jill's saddle to wipe out as much of their trail as possible, he felt a resurgence of confidence. He was all in one piece, and he had Grant's girl. He could bargain her for a whole skin.

They stopped for a meal of hard tack, and McCord unfastened the thongs that held Jill captive. He lifted her to the ground and stood apart from her quickly. He had an abnormal dislike of women, and close contact had always been repugnant to him. He stared at Jill out of black, glittering eyes.

'Now, Miss,' he said. 'If you want to see Grant again, you just do like I say now. All I want is to get to Huggett in Nebraska to pick up what belongs to me. If I do that, I'll leave you there safe and sound for Grant to catch up. If Grant catches up first, I'll trade you for me to go where I want unhindered. So the sooner we get there the better. Is that clear?'

Jill looked frankly into McCord's face, and she knew she had nothing to fear other than a quick dispatch if she was of no further use to him. Things could have been far worse. She settled for her good luck.

'I'll do like you say, Mister – er–' she replied simply.

'The name's McCord,' he replied. 'Now that you've given your word you can take off for a few minutes and see to your needs.'

Thankful for his delicacy, Jill made her way to cover, and when she returned McCord shared the hard tack with her; as they remounted, she put her hands behind her back, expecting to be tied. The act showed up the bulge in front of her jacket, and McCord thrust his hand inside, taking out the Derringer. He grinned and said, 'No need to tie you up now, I guess, that way we'll get to Nebraska all the quicker.'

Jill muttered her thanks and to McCord's satisfaction they travelled at a faster pace, but Jill was still one thought ahead; as they travelled, she reached behind her, lifting the dragging blanket, leaving the trail intact for Steve to follow.

Mid-day saw them over the Kansas river and McCord was quietly content. Two more days would see him home and dry. He was so concerned with plotting the route that he failed to smell out the Indians on the hills, keeping the two riders under constant surveillance. He was unprepared also for Eb Faulkner who rode out from behind a huge outcrop. Faulkner's eyes slid from McCord to Jill, and he licked his lips as he took in the shape of her.

'See you got away, then,' Faulkner sneered. 'Got yourself a nice prize too. I guess we can share her on the way to collect what's ours.'

Cold fury seethed in McCord, but he held on. 'How come you got away?' he asked.

'Guess I was lucky,' Faulkner replied. 'Mordant got clear too, but he tried to be sassy, so I cashed in his chips for him. That just leaves you and me, and like I said, you and me can share the girl and the dinero, or if you'd prefer we can go for broke now.'

Jill was filled with horror at the turn of fate. Faulkner made no attempt to disguise his intentions for her and she waited with bated breath for McCord's reaction. It came quickly. McCord's eyes glittered and his face was impassive as he looked full at Faulkner.

'Rubbing out Mordant's set your ambition too high, Faulkner,' he snapped. 'I share nothing with you, so go for those guns.'

Faulkner went into what he thought was slick action, but he was too late, a lifetime too late. He pitched out of the saddle, and McCord replaced his smoking gun and waved Jill on to resume their journey. She gave the corpse a glance of revulsion, and followed McCord more happily than she would have thought possible.

At sundown Jill felt the need for a hot drink and a meal but McCord would not permit a fire, and she had to be satisfied with water and hard tack. When she made to unfasten her saddle-roll McCord stopped her. 'Just let 'em graze, then we'll carry on. I want to cross the Nebraska line tomorrow.'

McCord reckoned on Grant resting up from sundown to sun-up, so by pushing on tonight they should make the cache without Grant on his heels.

They crossed into Nebraska, and the second night they rested. Then with just two hours of daylight left on the next day, they skirted the little township of Huggett and headed into the dying sun downgrade to a long, low valley. Gaining the valley, McCord led the way through shoulder-high grass to a thick copse of redwoods and beyond, where an overgrown compound almost covered a big log cabin. Hardly sparing a glance for the cabin, McCord pressed on towards the wall of precipitous cliffs about a mile distant.

Crossing a well-rutted, rough road, they rode along the face of the cliffs, then at length McCord stopped and gazed at the gaping black hole of a cave. He walked inside, motioning imperiously to Jill to stay where she was, and as she waited, he made his way into the cavern. Lighting matches, he rounded the corner and carefully picked his way for a hundred yards until he came up against a heavy wooden door. With the light of another match, he saw the locks and chains were intact, and with elation rising in him he picked his careful way out.

Jill was almost nodding from tiredness; and this fact, helped by the natural stealth of the Indian, contributed to her amazement when, opening her eyes with a start, she saw ten or twelve Indians ranged each side of the cave's mouth. Her first impulse was to scream, but a tall, hawk-faced brave placed a finger over his lips and held up the other hand in warning. She nodded her understanding, and the brave gave her the nearest approach to a smile that his impassive features would permit.

McCord emerged, blinking in the last of the day's light, and as he stepped clear of the cave he sensed danger. He went for his guns, then fell forward as a brave leapt in and clubbed him to the ground.

The braves closed in, tying McCord securely, then they slung him over his saddle and led him away. The chief waved for Jill to follow, and eventually they came to where their horses waited. Swinging lightly astride their lean, rangy mounts, the cavalcade headed for the less precipitous hillside.

Steve and Amos stared down at the grisly sight which was Eb Faulkner's corpse. The buzzards had been at work, and they circled angrily, waiting for the newcomers to move on.

'He came out from that gully,' Steve pointed out to Amos. 'Then palavered a while before going for the hardware.'

'So, that just leaves two of them,' Amos said flatly.

Steve nodded. 'Yeah, two of them and two of us. I reckon we can handle it from here on.'

'Yeah, I guess we can,' Amos agreed.

Painstakingly and doggedly, the two men stuck to their task of following the trail that dried up now and again, and, with three hours of daylight left on the second day, they were ten miles south of Huggett.

They followed the trail until, when they were just past Huggett, the light gave out, and the two men decided to camp. As they stripped the saddles from their mounts, five Indians rode up out of the murk, their hands raised in peace. Steve stepped away from Apache and returned the greeting. The leading Indian slid off his horse and by speech, sign and mime made Steve understand that a girl and a man had been made prisoner, and he was to take Steve and Amos to the chief, Ogalla, where the prisoners were held.

Steve turned to Amos to explain but he was already re-saddling. 'I understood enough of that,' he said with a grin, and Steve smiled to himself as he, also, re-saddled. When they were ready, the Indians turned their mounts and led the way.

For between four and five hours they rode, moving deeper and deeper into the hills that loomed over the Nebraskan plain, until they saw the pinpoints of light that were the fires of Ogalla's camp.

Ogalla stood outside his tepee, braves ranged either side of him as the little cavalcade rode in. The Indian who had led the party slid from his pony and spoke to Ogalla, indicating Steve and Amos. Ogalla glanced at the pards and nodded to the brave, indicating satisfaction, then the chief stepped forward to where Steve and Amos sat their mounts like statues.

'Welcome to the camp of Ogalla, Mister Grant and Mister Amos,' he said in excellent English. 'You wear the eagle feathers from Sequoia, son of Bald Eagle, and you bring honour to our camp.'

'It is we who are honoured, Ogalla,' Steve replied. His gaze swept around the perimeter of light for sight of Jill, but there was no sign of her. 'You have a white woman captive?' he asked.

Ogalla shook his head. 'Not captive, Mister Grant. She sleeps in her tepee. The captive is the man McCord. He is under guard until tomorrow, when he will pay for his crimes against the Sioux nation.'

Amos climbed down from his mount and stood facing Ogalla, his face grimly serious. 'If you intent McCord to die, it should not matter to you how he dies. For six moons I have followed him to kill him with these,' Amos spread his hands, then continued, 'I will feel cheated if he dies any other way.'

Ogalla looked long and hard into the negro's face, noting the long scars that ran the length of it, and plumbing the intensity of feeling that burned in his eyes, he placed a hand on Amos' shoulder.

'You know that once you start in mortal combat it would have to be to the death, whoever wins?' and when Amos nodded, 'Go to your tepee now, both of you and sleep. We will palaver and let you know in the morning.'

Amos murmured his thanks, then followed Steve, who headed for a tepee in the wake of the Indians who had brought them into camp. Steve wanted to remonstrate with Amos, to persuade him to leave Mc-Cord's punishment to the Sioux, but he decided to say nothing. Amos had inalienable right to extract revenge, so instead, he built smokes for each of them before settling down to sleep.

When they emerged from their tepee in the morning, the camp was alive. Ogalla sat in front of his tepee and called them to join him. McCord was sat opposite, eating pemmican mechanically, guarded by six braves. His eyes glittered with hatred as he glanced at Steve but the young Texan ignored him. Ogalla passed strips of pemmican to the pardners, and waited for them to eat before looking at Amos and saying, 'We palavered, and you can do battle. In one hour all will be ready.'

Amos smiled and nodded his pleasure, and Steve, when he met the glance his pard flashed at him, tried to look confident; then, asking Ogalla's permission, he took Amos aside and tried to impress upon him all the dirty tactics McCord would employ in the fight for survival, but Amos quietened him and said, 'Don't fret none, Steve. He can do what he wants but he'll never escape these.' And again he spread his hands.

The hour passed and work stopped in the camp. Braves and squaws came from all quarters and formed in groups, eyeing the two men who would soon be locked in combat. While they gathered, Steve looked for Jill, hoping that she would be spared the spectacle, but it seemed she still slept, and he was thankful.

Ogalla called Amos to the centre of the thickly packed ring, and told him to take off his boots, while the braves beside McCord divested him of his footwear; then the chief motioned the two men together. McCord glared across at Steve before moving to the middle, pure venom in his glance. 'So – Grant! When it comes to the showdown, you hide behind an old man!'

Before Steve could answer Amos broke in. 'I was the only man you left alive at the Billon's near Wayneboro, McCord, and I swore to follow you to Hell and back until I'd choked the life out of you. Grant is standing back, and the Sioux nation is standing back, because they reckon I've got first claim.'

McCord looked at the middle-aged negro with a sneer on his lips, then he hurled himself at Amos, taking him unawares, sending him crashing to the ground, then McCord was swarming all over him, throwing savage punches at the head and throat.

Steve felt a feathery touch as someone squeezed in beside him, and he looked down at Jill's lovely but anxious face. Involuntarily his arm went around her, and he hugged with all the pent-up anxiety of the last couple of days. She looked up and saw the answer to her hopes clearly showing in his eyes and expression. Only one thing now clouded their future, the fight, with Amos in deadly combat. Holding each other tight, they watched, praying for advantage to the old negro.

McCord broke away from Amos, throwing a handful of dust into his eyes, then jumped in, stomping his heel time and again into his adversary's face. He tried it once too often and Amos caught his leg, and with a heavy twist brought McCord down. Amos held on, and despite McCord's threshing feet, he clawed his way up McCord's torso. As they got level McCord thumped savage blows into Amos' face but at last the negro's hands closed around McCord's neck. McCord's blows rained with increased force and savagery but Amos' grip grew tighter, and stayed, despite everything McCord tried.

McCord's evil mind became a searing, blinding kaleidoscope of pictures as the blood supply to his brain drained away. Indian squaws, carrying their papooses, fleeing in terror, and in vain. Young children with eyes wide open with unadulterated fear, being cut down like chaff. Drugged and drunken braves butchered where they lay, and the leaping flames from Southern mansions showering sparks skywards, each conflagration a funeral pyre for the charnel house he had created. These pictures faded, leaving one image in front of him, the negro Amos, the livid scars a monument to his own evil; then, like a background to Amos, three pictures of Steve Grant jostled for prominence in the background. In the saloon at Waco, in the store at Waco and riding in to confront him with Udell's corpse for burial; and the cool, unafraid face mocked him.

In a rush of realization McCord felt death imminent, and his brain tried to summon every last reserve of strength to tear away the negro's grip, but his brain was no longer able to send messages to his weakening body. His blows slowed down, and his struggling died away, until at last he lay inert. A full minute later, at a sign from Ogalla, two braves stepped forward and prised Amos' hands away, and helped the negro to his feet.

Jill gave a shudder of relief and turned her face into Steve, who held her tight before going forward to meet Amos. He looked into Amos' bloodied face, then hugged him and led him back to Ogalla. The chief grasped Amos' hand and led him to his own tepee. A few minutes later they came out again. Amos' face now cleaned of blood, and ceremoniously, Ogalla gave to the smiling negro the treasured, crossed eagle feathers that gave him protection wherever the Plains Indians held sway.

McCord's corpse was dragged away, and Ogalla had his braves lined up when the pards and Jill were saddled up ready to leave. As they rode out of the camp the braves held spears aloft in salute, and Jill led the way towards the cave where McCord had cached the stolen Southern property.

'Well,' said Steve when they were alone, 'That just leaves one, Mordant.'

'Mordant!' Jill exclaimed. 'No – he's dead! The man McCord killed on the trail, I think his name was Faulkner, said he'd killed Mordant himself.'

Steve pulled up Apache, and Amos and Jill reined in and looked at him questioningly. 'That being so, we can leave what's hidden in that cave for those with a right to fight over it. I guess it's time we lived our own lives. I've got a ranch in Texas where you, Amos, can be my right-hand man, and there's a man in Texas who'll maybe give his permission for me to wed his daughter.'

A cloud crossed Jill's features until she saw Steve's smile.

'Yeah – his name's Rankin,' Steve added.

They turned to the south, and as Amos dropped behind the lovers, he touched the crossed feathers in his hat, and pride filled his battered frame.

The publishers hope that this book has given you enjoyable reading. Large Print Books are especially designed to be as easy to see and hold as possible. If you wish a complete list of our books please ask at your local library or write directly to:

The Golden West Large Print Books
Magna House, Long Preston,
Skipton, North Yorkshire.
BD23 4ND

This Large Print Book, for people
who cannot read normal print,
is published under the auspices of

THE ULVERSCROFT FOUNDATION

... we hope you have enjoyed this book.
Please think for a moment about those
who have worse eyesight than you ...
and are unable to even read or enjoy
Large Print without great difficulty.

You can help them by sending a
donation, large or small, to:

**The Ulverscroft Foundation,
1, The Green, Bradgate Road,
Anstey, Leicestershire, LE7 7FU,
England.**
or request a copy of our brochure for
more details.

The Foundation will use all donations
to assist those people who are visually
impaired and need special attention
with medical research, diagnosis
and treatment.

Thank you very much for your help.